D1505199

# The NOT-SO-PerFecT PLAN

**Books by Christina Matula**
**available from Inkyard Press**

*The Not-So-Uniform Life of Holly-Mei*
*The Not-So-Perfect Plan*

# THE NOT-SO-PERFECT PLAN

inkyard PRESS

**CHRISTINA MATULA**

ISBN-13: 978-1-335-42917-9

The Not-So-Perfect Plan

For questions and comments about the quality of this book, please contact us at CustomerService@Harlequin.com.

Inkyard Press
22 Adelaide St. West, 41st Floor
Toronto, Ontario M5H 4E3, Canada
www.InkyardPress.com

Printed in U.S.A.

For Jukka, Elsa, and Sandor.

And to my friends in Hong Kong, past and present—you were my family when far from home.

MAP OF HONG KONG
NEW TERRITORIES
EIGHT IMMORTALS TRAIL
Tsing Yi
KOWLOON
Hong Kong Museum of History
TSIM SHA TSUI
Victoria Park
Causeway Bay
CENTRAL
The Peak
Man Mo Temple
Wan Chai
HONG KONG ISLAND
LANTAU ISLAND BIG BUDDHA
Deep Water Bay
Ocean Park
Repulse Bay
Tai Tam Prep
Big Wave Bay
Dragon's Back Trail
Shek O
Stanley
Middle Island
Lamma Island

# 1

The crack of my field hockey stick sends the ball up the length of the pitch. I sprint to join the action and yell, "Square left." Without needing to look up, my right wing knows exactly where I am—we are in sync. I receive her pass, step into the shooting circle, the D, and prepare my shot. I lunge low as I flip my stick over and execute a perfect reverse hit of the ball. It thumps against the backboard and the trill of the umpire's whistle signals my goal. My heart soars. The mix of high fives and pats on the back I get from fellow Tai Tam Prep players signals that I belong in this new school and new city.

A few minutes later, I'm in the shooting circle again, dribbling around a defender from the British International

School. She tries to sweep the ball away, but I force a foul and it hits her foot, earning us a penalty corner—in field hockey, the ball can never ever touch your foot, unless you're the goalie. Just like hands in soccer. I look up at Mr. Chapman, aka Coach Chappie, and he gives me the signal for play number 1, indicating a push out from me to the top of the shooting circle, where Saskia Okoh, our star striker, will take a simple shot. Our team huddles, I tell the team the plan, and everyone nods. I plant my feet and give a strong, solid push out to Saskia, and like every penalty shot she takes, she scores. As cheering erupts, the half-time whistle blows.

"Great goal," I say to Saskia as we run back to the side-lines for our mid-game chat. She smiles and thanks me.

We gather around Coach Chappie, who wields his white-board and marker like the conductor of an orchestra. We watch, mesmerized by the flying Xs and Os as he directs the plan to defend our lead and seal our win.

"Nice goal on the reverse stick, Holly-Mei," Coach says. I smile proudly. Being center-midfield, I don't score that often, and I even got to use a fancy shot.

"And textbook goal, Saskia. That's surely the Golden Stick award for you," he says, referring to the prize awarded to each division's top scorer of the season.

I'm happy for Saskia. I only wish there could be a prize for people who assist with the goals, too, like when I earned us that penalty corner she scored on. As if reading my mind, Coach says to the rest of us, "MVP for the season is still up for grabs, so give it your all for the last half of the game." I smile and nod. I guess things I do count after all. Maybe that's the prize I should be thinking about, MVP, Most Valuable Player. I wonder if I even have a chance.

The whole of the second half, the other team tries to get close to our goal, but our midfield and defensive lines are just too strong. We press forward relentlessly into their D. With one minute left on the clock, the umpire awards us a penalty corner for dangerous play. This is going to be our last short corner of the season and it would be amazing to end with another goal. I look to Coach and he signals play number 1, just like before. I'm annoyed that he wants me to pass it to Saskia again. We're going to win anyway, so shouldn't someone else have a turn to shine? But I do as he says and of course she scores.

A few of the parents come over to the team bench to help us celebrate the end of the field hockey season. Millie, my younger sister, opens a large rectangular box to reveal a cake she baked shaped like crossed field hockey sticks. Millie is a fantastic cook and I love trying all her kitchen experiments.

"I was going to write City Champions on the sticks but then I remembered you're only in second place," she says.

"Now, now. You girls had a great season and second place in the league is quite the accomplishment," Dad says.

Mom nods and says, "That's absolutely right."

Saskia's parents are there too. Mrs. Okoh opens a bottle of sparkling apple juice. "Here are some celebratory bubbles for Saskia's Golden Stick award," she says as she pours us each a cup. She looks at her daughter's confused face and says, "I calculated and you've secured it by eight goals. That's my little champion."

Saskia's brown cheeks flush red. I pass her a piece of cake and roll my eyes, trying to show her I understand how embarrassing parents can be.

"Eleanor, is it true you used to play field hockey internationally?" Mom asks Saskia's mother.

"Yes, for Great Britain." She pops her sunglasses on top of her blond hair.

"No wonder Saskia is so skilled," Dad says in admiration.

"Did you ever play in the Olympics?" I ask.

Her smile freezes and she pushes her sunglasses back over her eyes and sighs. "I was a reserve but didn't get to go to Atlanta in the end."

Mr. Okoh chimes in with a big smile, "But if Holly-Mei

13

teaches Saskia how to do a reverse stick goal, our daughter might have her own chance at the Olympics."

"Dad—" Saskia starts to say, shaking her head.

"I'm just joking, pumpkin," he says with a wink.

Players start to leave slowly and it's just our two families left. Millie is taking selfies in the stands; Dad and Saskia's mom are chatting about London, where they're both from; Mom and Saskia's dad talk about work since they're at the same big company, Lo Holdings International, and both have a fancy title that tells me nothing about what they actually do.

"You girls should get together over the holidays," Dad says. "We're staying in town, too."

The parents turn to us expectantly. Saskia and I look at each other and shrug. "I guess so," we say in unison. It's not that I don't like Saskia, but I don't really know her that well. We're not in any of the same classes so we're only together when we play and practice with the Tai Tam Prep junior field hockey team. She seems to live and breathe the sport, even training and playing with a team at a top local club, so we haven't met up at Stanley Plaza or Repulse Bay Beach, where all the students hang out. I wonder if she has other interests. I wouldn't mind becoming friends with her. I feel like we have an unspoken connection because she's mixed-race like me. Her parents are both British; her mom is white and her dad is Black. She's beautiful—like a teen Zendaya but with curlier hair and a smattering of golden freckles.

I gather my stick bag and our family heads to the van where Ah-Lok, our driver, is waiting at the side of the King's Park stadium to take us back to Hong Kong Island from the Kowloon side. I am still surprised about the fact that we have a driver. Our life has changed so much since we moved to Hong Kong from Toronto five months ago. Not least of which, I'm wearing a hockey skirt and short sleeves outside in the December sunshine. I'm sure my friends back home are already in woolen tuques and mitts.

"Wait, I forgot my mouth guard." I jump out of the van and race back through the stadium gates. Saskia is leaning on the fence and it looks like she and her parents are in the middle of a serious discussion. I keep my eyes on the ground as I pass but I can't help but hear what they're saying.

"We need to get you extra sessions with your private coach over the Christmas holidays," her father says.

"But you said I could take a break from hockey. That I could do that online animation camp," Saskia says.

"If you want to be an elite player and make the Olympics, you need to prioritize training and sacrifice hobbies," her mother says.

My eyes flick upward at them. Saskia's shoulders are

stooped and she's staring at her feet. I feel bad for her. I thought my mom had high expectations for me, but this is next-level.

The following day at school, no one can concentrate in anticipation of our upcoming two-week Christmas break. At least in the afternoon, we have the Grade 7 Winter Holiday Party. My cousin Rosie and I position ourselves by the large table filled with the various baked goods each student has brought in.

"Oh my, this spiced shortbread is scrummy," she says.

"Millie helped me bake them," I say. "It was her idea to add the star anise."

"I should save one for Henry before they're all gone," she says as she piles another on her plate. Henry Lo is a cute boy in our grade, and lately Rosie has spent a lot of time studying with him. "How I wish you were coming with us to Thailand. It would make it so much more fun. Now I have to hang out with my brother for two weeks," Rosie says, referring to her twin, Rhys, and rolls her eyes.

"I wish we could go, too. I've never been to Thailand," I say wistfully, thinking about all the delicious food she'll get to eat, like pad Thai and mango sticky rice. But Mom said she couldn't take that much time off work. We moved here for my mother's big promotion, which keeps her busier and traveling more than ever before. I'm super proud of her, although it's confusing when people assume we moved for my dad's job instead of hers. This new job came with lots of new things, like instead of living in a bungalow and driving around in our Toyota, we live in a big apartment, or *flat* as they say in Hong Kong, right on the beach in Repulse Bay and have a driver. We even have a housekeeper, called a *helper* here, named Joy, who right now is abroad visiting her family for Christmas. She makes better pancakes than Dad—she laughed when we told her, but we don't have the heart to tell him.

Dad has always been home more than Mom, and when we came here, he took a leave of absence from teaching at the university. He's writing a novel—I don't think he's actually started writing it yet though, but he has papers, articles, and notes piled everywhere. He calls it research. Mom jokingly calls it procrastination.

As Rosie, my friends, and I gobble up all the Christmas goodies, everyone talks about the exotic beaches and swish ski slopes they'll be jetting off to for the holidays.

"I can't wait to hit the powder in Verbier," Henry says with a huge grin, his braces glinting.

"We're planning to wake up early every day and be the first ones on the piste to make fresh tracks," Theo says. They are cousins and spending Christmas together.

"Next year, you must join our family at our chalet in Hokkaido. The powder in Japan is the best," Gemma says. "And where are you off to?" she asks, turning to the rest of us.

"Down Under. I've never been to Australia, I'm so excited. It'll be a summer Christmas for me," Rainbow says.

"Oh, I hope you get to see a koala! And we're going on a cruise up the Vietnamese coast," Snowy says.

Gemma's eyes rest on me. I didn't realize everyone was leaving for the holidays.

"We're just staying here. I'm sure it will be fun to explore Hong Kong now that the weather is not sauna-level hot," I say.

"I'm sure you'll have a brilliant time," Rosie says with her usual cheeriness and she passes me a treat off her plate.

With everyone gone, two weeks is going to feel so long, but I'm sure my friends and I will be messaging and sharing photos all day, every day.

The first few days of break pass quickly. While Mom works, Millie, Dad, and I potter around the markets in Mongkok for flowers and festive trinkets to decorate our flat. Yesterday, we took the Star Ferry over to the Cultural Centre, a big brown building that looks like a giant skateboard ramp, and saw a matinee of *The Nutcracker* ballet, followed by a family dinner at one of the fancy hotels along the water. I texted Rosie a photo of me with the lead ballerina after the show and she texted me back with a starry-eyed emoji. Her dream is to be a dancer with the Royal Ballet in London.

Tonight, I text her some photos of our visit to the Ten Thousand Buddhas Monastery in Sha Tin. I didn't believe at first that there were really 10,000 Buddha statues and I tried to count, but I lost track after 500. While I wait for her reply, I check out my friends' Instagram stories. I don't usually post—I just like to observe. My best friend in Toronto, Natalie, has posted a video of her and some kids in my old neighborhood out tobogganing. Henry and his cousin Theo Fitzwilliam-Lo are together in Switzerland—there are videos of them carving fresh powder on their skis. Snowy Wong is on a cruise in Vietnam with her grandmother and has been posting amazing footage of limestone cliffs. There are photos of Rainbow Hsieh climbing Sydney Harbour Bridge and Gemma Tsien with her puppy Cookie inside her father's company jet. I send a text to our group chat: *Loving all your photos. Keep them coming!* I scroll through my phone to see if there's something I should share, but nothing seems as cool and exciting as what they're doing. Instead, I wait for them to ask me about my holiday. And I wait. And wait some more. Even though I can tell that everyone has seen my message, no one replies. I guess everyone is too busy having fun.

Two days later, I still don't have any replies, but people are continually posting about their trips. I even see that Rosie's latest story features her on the beach with a girl I recognize from a different grade at school.

That afternoon, I'm finally able to connect with her on FaceTime.

"Oh, it's so lovely," Rosie gushes. "There are quite a few families from Tai Tam Prep here, so we're all hanging out. How about you?"

"Just doing family stuff," I say. "I found a new bubble tea place in Causeway Bay."

I hear someone knock at her hotel room door. "I'm sorry, but I've got to go. A bunch of us are going to an elephant sanctuary. Call you later, okay?"

"Sure, okay," I say, a little disappointed at our less-than-two-minute catch-up.

I walk toward Millie's room. Maybe I can convince her to go for a walk along the boardwalk. She's at her desk on a multi-friend video call. I hear laughter and people saying things like, *I know, right*, and *I can't believe it*. She waves me over and introduces me to the girls from her Grade 6 class that I don't know. Then she sends me away with a request to return with a plate of cookies. I ignore that and just curl up on the sofa with one of the books I got for Christmas.

Rosie and I manage to connect again on FaceTime a few days later. She tells me all about the Thai cooking class she did with the family.

"That sounds so fun. We went on a bicycle tour in Yuen Long and got to cross the river in an old-style rowboat. Millie almost fell in, bike and all," I say. Rosie giggles. It's nice to finally chat. But then she says, "Oh wait, Henry's calling. Would you mind if I answered it?"

"No problem," I say and paste on a smile so she doesn't know that it bothers me. Not only is she hard to pin down but she also drops me so quickly.

Hearing about her cooking class has made me hungry and I head to the kitchen for a snack. Millie is already there and the kitchen is filled with the strong smell of cheese.

"What are you doing?" I ask.

"I'm making a fondue with Lizzie," she says. She's on a FaceTime with Henry's little sister. Lizzie waves at me from the phone screen. They both love cooking and have been regularly cooking together remotely over the break. "I can pretend I'm in Switzerland too," she says as she dips bread in the creamy gooey liquid.

Even though Millie's friends are all away, she doesn't seem to be left out of anything. I even texted Saskia the other day to see if she wanted to go see a movie, but she was too busy with extra field hockey coaching sessions.

I pull my phone out of my pocket and check it again. It feels heavier now. Other than a short reply or two to my questions about everyone's holidays, there have been no new messages since yesterday. It's like these last couple of weeks, everyone has completely forgotten about me.

# 2

I wake up on New Year's Day—the first day of a new calendar year, in a new home, in a new country. There are so many benefits linked to being new. *Shiny and new. New and improved.* Now that I'm not the new girl anymore, is being regular Holly-Mei Jones, field hockey player and bubble tea enthusiast, enough to keep my friends from completely forgetting about me?

My sleep was fitful, restless, and I feel exhausted. I hide my phone with still unanswered texts under my pillow and pull my duvet over my head to block out the sun. The mornings are brighter this time of year compared to back in Toronto. But I shouldn't compare things to how they were back in Canada.

I take a long shower, hoping to wash off the cloud of

gray thoughts about unresponsive friends that are hovering over my head. Afterwards, I sit at my desk and open my laptop, pressing the video icon beside Ah-ma's name. As soon as my grandmother's gentle smiling face fills the screen, the tightness in my chest loosens. I take a deep breath.

"Ah-ma." I let it linger like a balm in the air.

"Baobei," Ah-ma says, *my treasure*. "Happy New Year!"

The biggest change in our home has been leaving Ah-ma, my Taiwanese grandmother, my mom's mom. She had lived with us ever since Ah-gong, my grandfather, passed away and I feel a tug in my chest whenever I think of her still in Toronto instead of here with us. Ah-ma said Hong Kong was far away from her friends and was too hot for her (it is soooo hot and humid here, but it's finally cooled to a nice temperature), and that Mom's brother, Uncle Eli, and his wife, Auntie Julia, needed her help with the new baby. I tried not to be mad at them for keeping Ah-ma from moving with us, even though she said it was her choice to stay behind, but when I signed their Christmas card, I made a point of not putting *xoxo* beside my name.

"Happy New Year's Eve!" I say. We are thirteen hours ahead of her. "Are you busy?" I can see that she's in Uncle Eli's kitchen and there are people behind her.

"Never busy for you. I have few minutes before broth

is ready. We're having huo guo, so I don't have to cook, just chopping."

Hot pot, my favorite winter food. Even though it's morning here, my mind fills with thoughts of the steaming broth in which I get to dunk and cook my own dumplings and meatballs.

"Baobei?" Ah-ma brings me back from my imagined feast. "What did you do for New Year?"

"We did a hike on Lantau Island. I thought Hong Kong would be all city—concrete and skyscrapers, but there are so many country parks and islands to explore. We walked to this little fishing village where all the houses are on stilts. It was so cool. And we found a bakery with the best Chinese doughnuts. Millie says she's going to try and make sa yong at home." My mouth starts to water at the thought of the golden crispy dough lightly sprinkled with sugar, still warm to the touch. Millie's like one of those super talented musicians that can replicate a song just by hearing it once, but she does that with food. And a bit of help from the internet.

"Sounding delicious," Ah-ma says. I hear a baby cry in the background and that's probably my cue to let her go.

"Well, I just wanted to hear your voice. It's the last day before I have to go back to school." I let out a big sigh.

"I thought things good at school?"

"Yes, they are great," I say with exaggerated sunniness. "I just want them to stay that way." My stomach knots like it did when Ah-ma caught me in a lie about who ate a piece of the surprise birthday cake—my denials were undone by the evidence of a chocolate crumb mustache over my lip. But if things really are so great, why isn't my phone pinging with messages like Millie's?

"Remember, you have found sweetness. But life cannot be sweet all the time," Ah-ma says.

"I know, I know. Give hugs to the kids for me." We blow each other kisses and I hang up the phone.

Outside the living room, I step onto the balcony overlooking Repulse Bay and the open sea. My clenched stomach instantly relaxes. The view of the crescent beach and the sparkling water always brightens my mood. The morning sun on my skin feels like it's giving me a hug. I can make out some open water swimmers with their orange safety buoys heading to Middle Island. I hope I can try that soon.

Mom is setting the dining table and I can tell from the smell that Dad is in the kitchen making his famous fluffy pancakes with a side of bacon.

"Last day of holidays today," Mom says in a singsong voice. She touches my shoulder. "I hope you weren't too disappointed we weren't able to travel to Thailand with your cousins."

"No, it's okay. I know you had to work. Plus, it was nice to explore the city, just the four of us."

"Thank you." She pats my hand. "Now go see how your dad is getting on with those pancakes and I'll try and wake your sister up."

In the kitchen Dad flips a pancake and it lands perfectly on top of a stack on the serving plate.

"Good morning, poppet, and a Happy New Year to you!" he chirps as if he's the happiest bird in the world. Dad loves birds. We got him a *Birds of Hong Kong* puzzle for Christmas and it's taken over the dining table, but luckily the table is big enough for ten people, so we can shift it to one end. He puts the platter of pancakes and crispy bacon, along with the steaming pot of coffee, onto a tray and heads to the dining room.

I grab the maple syrup from the fridge. I was excited to find it in the grocery store downstairs in our apartment complex, Lofty Heights. Now, we'll always have the sweet taste of our old home in our new home.

Millie shuffles to the table in her unicorn slippers and yawns with exaggerated movements, hands in the air, before plopping down loudly into a chair. Mom raises an eyebrow. "Amelia-Tian, is everything alright?"

She manages an indistinguishable *hmph* before stabbing her fork into a stack of pancakes. "It's so early. It's not even eight o'clock!"

"Well, we have to be up even earlier tomorrow, so we'd better get used to it," I say between mouthfuls.

Millie rolls her eyes. "Always so logical, Holly-Mei," she says like it's a bad thing.

"She's right, poppet," says Dad, as I nod along.

Millie sighs and picks up a piece of bacon with her fingers and dips it into a pool of maple syrup. "Fiiiine."

The day passes in a slow, lazy Sunday kind of way. I help Millie try out a new recipe she invented for candy cane-White Rabbit chip cookies. We each lick one of the mixing blades before Mom catches us and scolds us for eating raw batter.

Millie packs a dozen cookies into a container to share with her friends at school tomorrow.

"Do you want to bring some too?" she asks. Sometimes she surprises me with her thoughtfulness.

"Sure, thanks." I pack the other half of the batch, smiling as I imagine the crew at lunch eagerly gathering around my Tupperware. No one's going to forget about me now. I pop a leftover White Rabbit candy in my mouth, the delicate rice paper coating sticking to my palate before I bite down, releasing a burst of sweet creamy goodness.

My phone trills just as I'm going to bed—it's almost nine

o'clock. On a Sunday! But when I see Natalie's name flash on my screen, I jump across the bed to grab it. We squeal excited greetings before diving into our holiday recap.

"We went to Ottawa and skated on the Rideau Canal. It's the longest skating rink in the world. It was fun, but minus twenty degrees Celsius with the wind!" Natalie says.

I shiver at the thought of being so cold. "Then you're not going to want to hear that I was wearing a T-shirt almost every day." We both laugh. "What else did you do?" I ask.

"I got lots of gift cards for Christmas, so Ellie, Katie, and I checked out the sales at the Eaton Centre. Katie has a crush on Noah and when he arrived at the mall, she totally ditched us so she could hang out with him."

"Really? That's so annoying."

"It really was. I don't know why people change when they have crushes."

We talk a bit more about people back in Toronto and then move on to how much we're dreading going back to school.

"We have to start algebraic equations. Yuck," Natalie says.

"Oh, we did that last term. They're so easy," I say dismissively.

There's a distinct pause before she speaks again.

"Holly-Mei—"

I know that tone. It's a *filter your thoughts* kind of tone. A *don't always blurt out what pops in your head* kind of tone. A *think of how others might feel* kind of tone. Images of me in the cafeteria at Maple Grove Elementary during summer camp last year flash through my head. Me, standing with a container full of rainbow-sprinkled cupcakes to offer my friends, but instead getting berated about how I open my big mouth too much or need to be flexible or think of others' feelings—and my face heats up with both embarrassment and shame.

"Sorry. Old habits die hard." I smile meekly. "How's this? We started them last term. They're not so bad. You'll get the hang of it in no time."

"Better," she says with a smile and a nod.

We chat and laugh until Mom knocks on my door, saying lights out.

After baking with Millie and packing my sure-to-be-loved cookies for my friends, I was sort of looking forward to the first day of school back from holidays. But chatting with Natalie and remembering what happened with the rainbow-sprinkled cupcakes—how no one even took one and how I ended up biking home and hiding them in the kitchen trash—I'm filled with more doubt than any number of candy cane-White Rabbit chip cookies can soothe.

# 3

It's only been a couple of weeks since school let out for Christmas break, but I let out a silent *wow* when the bus turns into the Tai Tam Prep campus. I forget my first-day-back-at-school insecurities as I admire the view. It's so different from Maple Grove Elementary, our single-story redbrick school back in Toronto. Tai Tam Prep has all these gleaming white columns, in what Dad says is Greek Revival style. One wing is the Lower School for kids up to Grade 6, Millie's grade. The other, larger wing is the Upper School, Grade 7 to 12. A giant banner in white and blue school colors flutters from the front congratulating all the sports teams that won championships in the autumn.

When he sees the rugby banner, my cousin Rhys, his normally pale skin pink and peeling from his beach holiday, stands up and gives a loud *woohoo*. The junior rugby team won the junior city league. I shoot him a look, not because I'm annoyed he's celebrating, but because he rips me from my daydreams and sends me back to my angst-filled reality. But of course he takes it the wrong way.

"Better luck next year, Holly-Mei. No banners for second place," Rhys says as he looks for a fellow player to high-five, but he doesn't find anyone. He's such a dork.

"Rhys, please cool it already," Rosie says to her twin brother as she shakes her head. Some of her silky blond hair falls from her ballet bun and she tucks it back in with a delicate, graceful movement. "He can be so annoying. Don't you worry—your hockey team will have its own banner in no time. Winning isn't everything." Rosie is always cheery and positive. I'm so happy she's back from her trip and we can hang out all day every day.

"Sure," I say with a shrug. "I don't care about the banner. The season was so much fun." As amazing as winning the junior league would have been, I'm going to take my time to practice and improve—I have my eye on an even bigger prize. Not just potentially MVP for this year, but in two years, when I'm in Grade 9, I'm going to try out for the Tai Tam Prep senior field hockey team. They get to play in tournaments in Bangkok and Singapore and have the option to train at summer camp in Holland. But the best part is that the girls on the team all hang out together and proudly wear their Tai Tam Prep Dragons Hockey hoodies around campus. I can't wait to be part of a cool, tight-knit group like that. I'd bet that they remember to text each other over the holidays.

I catch a glimpse of Theo and his cousin Henry as they get off the bus. Theo was the first Eurasian I met at Tai Tam Prep. We always joke that it takes one to know one. There are so many mixed-Asians and Asians at school and many of them have lived all over the world, not just Hong Kong. It's kind of neat being part of the majority for once, even though I've always loved my mixed-race background. I get the best of both worlds—I mean, who wouldn't want two sets of holidays to celebrate? Theo and I wave at each other before we're caught up in the sea of kids being ushered into school by the bus monitors.

Before I step inside, I turn to Rosie for a word of support or a little smile to help melt away my worries of the last couple of weeks. But she's not there—she's already beelining it to Henry's side. I can't believe she just left me without saying anything—it seems like she missed him so much but didn't miss me at all.

I walk into the lobby alone. The cacophony of excited students hits me like a giant auditory wave. I panic when I don't see anyone from our group, so I duck behind a column.

My heart feels like it's beating out of my chest and my face heats up. I touch my cheek with my hand to cool it down. *You're being silly*, I say to myself. *Go find your friends.* I take a few deep breaths to gather courage as I think about heading back to search for them. I'm hoping we can reconnect before class starts. As I step back into the crowd, I adjust the skirt of my school uniform. I'm still getting used to wearing a skirt—it's a huge departure from my favorite outfit of shorts or leggings and a T-shirt—but I like the idea of having a uniform. I never need to think about what I wear to school and no one is judging me on my clothes or where I buy them. No one is into brands, no one except Gemma Tsien, that is. And just like that, I spy Gemma, diamond earrings shimmering as she glides into the main entrance of the lobby clutching her huge Louis Vuitton bag.

I hesitate to approach her, especially as she's heading straight for Theo. Gemma and I are friends, but there's an edge to her whenever the two of us are around Theo. She says she's protective of him and their deep friendship—even their parents are friends—but I think she has a crush on him. I look around for a warmer, friendlier face. Rosie is still glued to Henry. Rhys and Jinsae Kim are chatting animatedly nearby with some of their rugby teammates. A few feet away, Snowy, her hair in a pearl-lined barrette, and Rainbow, with her Claudia Kishi-inspired top bun, are with a group of people in Grade 8 that I don't know—it looks like they have new older, cooler friends. As I watch from afar, my group of friends start to congregate around Gemma—she's passing out little gifts from her giant bag. After a few seconds of observing I take a step toward them.

I hear a chorus of *Oh hey, Holly-Mei*. But they all seem too busy holding, shaking, and cooing over the gifts to pay attention to me. They start opening the packages—delicate boxes of Royce' treats Gemma brought back from her ski trip to Hokkaido, Japan—and trading the little chocolate ganache squares so they end up with a variety box each.

"My father is friends with the owner and he sent a boxful of these limited-edition chocolates over to our chalet," Gemma explains to me.

"I don't think there's anything in that bag for me," I say, quoting Dorothy from *The Wizard of Oz*. I deliberately make it sound like a joke, but my stomach sinks.

A brief look of embarrassment flashes over her face. "Sorry, I didn't see you and forgot to save you something. Rhys ended up with two boxes. I can ask him to give you one."

"No worries, I ate too many chocolate Santas over the holidays," I say with a smile although I'm biting the inside of my cheek to keep my eyes from watering. I'm glad everyone else is too absorbed with their chocolates to notice me awkwardly standing there empty-handed.

Classes are a bit of a struggle—it's hard to sit still inside for so long, especially as I was hiking and outside much of the break. Thankfully, I'm too busy learning new things to think about forgetful friends. But when the lunch bell goes, instead of looking forward to eating, like usual, I don't have much of an appetite. Then I remember the treats that I brought with me. No one will be able to resist the candy cane-White Rabbit chip cookies—everyone will gather around me like they did Gemma this morning and things will be just like they were before the break.

Rosie and I both get steaming chicken pho and add a dash of chili oil before we take our seats at our group's regular spot in the atrium at the edge of the cafeteria. We're the first ones there. Right before we start to eat, I see a girl wave to get Rosie's attention.

"Sorry, I'll be right back. I just have to say hi." She gets up from the table and runs to the girl—the same person that was in her holiday Insta stories. My pho is too hot to eat yet, so I absentmindedly twirl one of my silver star earrings as I sit alone. Soon Rosie returns and the table fills back up with our group of friends. But something feels a bit off—people are either in side conversations with others I don't know or talking about things I'm not included in. Not to deliberately exclude me, but more because I wasn't around for the memories they're sharing. Normally, the warm broth of the pho mixed with the tang of the basil and mint are a delight to my taste buds, but everything seems bland today, even with the added chili sauce.

The container of cookies is in a cotton bag on my lap and I can't decide whether to pull them out. Maybe if I do, everyone will start chatting together warmly, just like we did before the break. Or maybe everyone is too busy cementing their friendships over things I don't seem to be a part of. I grip the bag and decide against it. I need to find something better than cookies to bring our group back together, tight, like we were last autumn.

After what feels like an extra-long day, the dismissal bell rings. I leave the container of cookies in my locker. Maybe I'll be brave enough to try tomorrow. A few steps away, Jinsae is surrounded by rolls of posters and he's tacking one to the bulletin board. It reads: *The Grade 7 Inter-School Tri Tournament Needs You!* With a cartoon panda pointing its finger at the reader.

"What's this?" I walk up and inspect the poster.

"It's a tournament the rugby team is helping to put on."

"A rugby tournament?"

"No, it's got something for everyone—swimming, running, and even a team event—the Dragon Dash. You can compete against other schools, win a prize, get some glory, that kind of thing."

I stay rooted, staring at the smiling panda. "Did you say a team event?"

"Yeah, the Dragon Dash is for teams of up to eight people. It's an orienteering race around the city. I gotta run and put these up before the late bus." He gathers his posters and darts down the hall before I can ask him more questions.

A team event? One where we can win a prize, get some

glory, together as friends? This is amazing. I'll ask them to join and things will definitely go back to how they were before the break. This is a completely and utterly perfect plan!

# 4

The next morning passes in a blur as my head works to absorb new things. In English class, we're going to start Shakespeare—the classic, tragic love story of *Romeo and Juliet*. Juliet is only thirteen years old, a few months older than me. I cannot imagine caring that much about a boy. But clearly, there are some people who do. I hear Gemma dreamily whisper to Snowy, her eyes fixed on Theo, "I hope we get to act out the play." I cover my mouth to muffle my giggle.

In math class, we review our homework on algebraic formulas. Easy peasy, like I told Natalie.

"Now class, please get into groups. We're going to explore real-life applications of what we just learned, like velocity, area, and profit," says Ms. Gurung.

I turn around to look for Rainbow but she's with some of the kids from her environment club. They're talking about trying to find the theoretical area of all the trash they collected off the beach last term. I sigh and turn instead to Rhys. Usually he's the one asking for my help, but he's already sitting with Jinsae and another rugby friend, excited about calculating the velocity of a drop kick.

"Holly-Mei, just squeeze in with one of the existing groups," says Ms. Gurung. But I don't want to squeeze into someone else's group like I'm sort of afterthought, a leftover.

"It's okay, I'll just do it on my own," I say.

But Ms. Gurung insists we all need to learn how to work with others and points at a table with two students. They are nice and move their chairs to make room for me. But I can't help feeling like I don't belong, especially as I look over at Rainbow and Rhys, laughing and smiling in their groups.

Morning break can't come soon enough. I step outside onto the school's roof terrace to get away from the humiliation of today's math class. I smile, the rays of sunshine hitting my face as I nibble on my snack, one of the candy cane-White Rabbit chip cookies from my locker. I'll have to tell Millie what a perfect combination the mint and milky toffee these are. I pinch myself as I scan my surroundings.

Within my 360-degree view, I have lush green mountains, the open sea, and a view of all the Tai Tam Prep sports facilities—swimming pool, soccer and rugby stadium, tennis courts, sailing club, and my favorite, the Smurf-blue field hockey pitch. It just takes a couple of deep breaths for me to relax.

I feel a gentle tap on my shoulder and I turn around, my face lighting up. Devinder Singh flicks his black wavy hair out of his eyes and flashes me his trademark megawatt smile.

"Hey Dev!" I'm excited to see him after more than two weeks. "What are you doing up here?"

"It's my happy place. Other than being on the actual hockey pitch." Dev is from Hong Kong so he says *hockey* as in *field hockey*, just like Rosie and everyone else here. Ice hockey is not really a thing in Hong Kong. There's only one full-sized rink in this city of seven and a half million people.

"I know—don't you love looking at this view?" I still can't believe how green Hong Kong is just minutes from downtown, and how much our campus looks like a mash-up of an Olympic training ground and a beach resort. "How was camp?" I ask. He's been away over the holidays with his hockey team at an elite training camp.

"We just got back last night. It was good. Hard-core. I learned some new tricks I can teach you!"

"Fantastic!" I say. Dev helped me perfect my reverse stick hit last autumn and he's the reason I scored that amazing goal. "When do you find out about the team for the Games?" His dream is to play for Hong Kong at the Junior Asian Games in the spring.

"The final squad will be announced soon. I'm so nervous."

"I'll keep my fingers crossed for you."

At noon, the cafeteria is humming with lunchtime chatter. I carry my bento box filled with rolls of salmon and cucumber maki and golden mixed-vegetable tempura and take a seat beside Jinsae, who is already tucking into his triple-decker club sandwich with rugby player-sized bites. I pop one of his sweet potato fries in my mouth as I greet him.

"Hey, hands off," he says, moving his hand to shield his tray. "I'm in training." He smiles and reaches into a bag of candy by his side. "Try this." He passes me one that is shaped like a banana. "I'm thinking of adding this to my import inventory."

Jinsae is Korean but has been living in Hong Kong since he was a baby. I used to think that Hong Kong would only be full of Chinese people, but there are so many other nationalities that make the city their home, too, just like Dev. Jinsae is starting a little business taking orders for Korean candy and using the money he makes to help pay for the rugby team trip to Australia at Easter for a big tournament. The rugby coach said that he expects the kids to work to pay for a share of their trip, even if parents are more than willing to cut a check and outright pay for everything.

"My halmoni, my grandmother, says these are really popular with all the kids back in Seoul," he says. "She'll send me more if people like them."

"I think real bananas are more my thing," I say, chewing on the soft candy with a banana-flavored center. "But, I'll take more of the grape gummies, the ones covered in chocolate."

"And the yakult-flavored ones," Rainbow says as she sits down beside me, her big silver hoop earrings glinting in the sunshine coming through the window. "But try and get the ones with less packaging." Rainbow is in the environment club at school and is always reminding us that we can do better, which I appreciate. Her family moved from California a few years ago and her mother started an environmental charity, so she knows a lot about how to be more eco-conscious. I'm relieved she's at our normal table and not with her environment friends from math class.

I remember the poster Jinsae was putting up yesterday. I need to find out how I can get all my friends to join and bring everyone back together.

"That tournament you mentioned—tell me more." I

rest my chopsticks on my tray and lean forward, ready to absorb everything.

Jinsae puts his sandwich down and his face lights up. "It's open to all Grade 7 students in the city and it's happening later this month. The first event is an open water swim from Repulse Bay Beach to Deep Water Bay Beach."

"Oh," I say, sitting back. "That's so far." I imagined that it would be just a few laps in the school's Olympic-sized swimming pool.

"It's just over three kilometers," Rainbow says. "Two miles, maybe." She swims a lot and has always been encouraging me to try open water swimming with her. I regret not taking her up on it before.

My eyes open wide. That's about sixty laps of the school pool. Jinsae picks up on my reaction and says, "Don't worry, it's a relay, with a swap at Middle Island yacht club."

"Phew!" I say. "What about the team event, the Dragon Dash?"

"It's a race all over the city with different clues based on history and sites. You can do it in a team of up to eight. And the last event is the race along the Eight Immortals Trail. You can run that in pairs, where they take your team's average time, or you can run it alone."

"Running with someone else sounds more fun," I say. *And less daunting*, I think.

"The points for each event are added to determine the winner," says Jinsae.

"And what does the winner get?" I ask. I'm hoping for a basket of all his Korean candy.

"My deepest appreciation, of course, since it's the first time the rugby team is putting this on. We're using the sponsorship funds to help with our Easter trip," he says. "Ms. Nguyen has asked me to write an article about the tournament and the participants for the school newspaper." Ms. Nguyen is the teacher supervisor for the *Tai Tam Prep Times*.

A big smile forms as I think about how I'll execute my perfect plan. I rub my blue-beaded bracelet that Rainbow made me last autumn. I'm sure she'd love being in the school paper to get more visibility for the environment club she co-chairs.

"Rainbow?"

"Hmmm?" she looks at me, her mouth full of pizza.

"Do you want to partner with me for this tournament?"

"Sounds interesting, but I have this eco-art project I'm working on with the environment club. It takes up a lot of my time so I won't have that much extra time to train."

"That's okay. We can work around your schedule. And you're already a fantastic swimmer—you won't need to train much. And I'm a decent runner. Plus, we'll be doing it just for fun."

"Well, then okay. Sounds super cool if it's just for fun."

"Perfect." It will be great to have a friend to do the swim and the run with. "And Jinsae, you'll join our Dragon Dash team, right? I'll order those banana gummies." I give him a playful nudge with my elbow.

"Sorry. I'm volunteering on all the race days, so I can't participate. But the other rugby guys can join." He nods his head toward the other end of the table.

I call out to Theo and Dev beside him, who both eagerly agree.

"I know my way around Hong Kong better than anyone, Holly-Mei," Gemma says from across the table as she flicks her shiny, bouncy, black hair.

Does she want to join too? I didn't think she would want to do anything that would involve lots of sweat and exertion. She always struck me as someone who preferred glamorous activities where she could be the star.

"Do you want to join the Dragon Dash team?" I ask.

Gemma straightens her back and loosens her pout. "Yes, I would love to. I can design our uniforms."

"Gems," Theo says. "It's a day running around the city. We don't need to dress up."

"Puh-lease, winners need to look like winners. Leave it to me. And I'll think of a good team name too."

I shrug. "Sure." I'm game for anything that will bring our group together again.

"Can I join too?" Rhys asks. He's always keen to join in anything that Gemma is part of.

"Sure. I'll ask Rosie too when she gets here." I definitely want her on the team so we can reconnect. It seems like every time I want to talk to her, she's always with Henry. They talk together at their lockers, sit together at lunch, and walk together to the bus. Thankfully, I still get to sit beside her on the bus, but I secretly worry that might change. A minute later, Rosie comes and sits beside me at our table, for once without Henry at her side. My chest fills with warmth when she agrees to join our team.

"What about Snowy?" Rainbow asks about her best friend. "She's doing a travel segment for her YouTube channel and I'm sure would love to film us running around." Snowy not only loves being in front of the camera but also behind it—one day she's going to be famous.

"Hey, I heard my name." Snowy sits down on the bench beside Rainbow and smooths out her silky hair. We explain the race to her and she starts excitedly rambling off all the camera angles she can get of us as we race around the city.

"Great. Our team for this tournament is sorted. Rainbow and I will do the swim relay and trail race, and the eight of us will do the Dragon Dash." I hear Rosie mumble something about "too bad there's no room for Henry," but everyone else cheers *woohoo*.

I pull out my container of cookies and everyone dives in and happily crunches away. I scan the table, my face beaming, my perfect plan in motion.

# 5

Later that week, I hesitate when I see Rosie and Henry huddled at her locker. I don't know if I should approach them, whether I'll be a third wheel. But Rosie sees me and waves me over and in the same second says goodbye to Henry, who walks toward the library.

"Oh, he's not coming to eat with us?" I ask. I must sound a bit snarky, although I don't mean to, because Rosie's mouth moves into a little O shape.

"Is everything okay, Holly-Mei?"

I want to say, "You seem to be stuck to Henry and I feel left out." But instead I just say, "Sure, what do you mean?"

That seems to appease her because right away she asks me about hanging out after school at her place and I feel silly for being so insecure. That feeling further evaporates when she links my arm in hers and we walk together to-ward the cafeteria. Rosie has an extra spring in her step compared to this morning.

"So, I just had performing arts—" Rosie says. She looks like she is about to burst with excitement.

"And?" I stop in the middle of the hallway and face her, my eyes quizzical. People swerve to avoid bumping into us.

"And Ms. Salonga asked me to be part of a perfor-mance."

"That's fantastic! A school performance?"

"Actually—" She bites her lip to temper the huge smile that is slowly spreading across her face. "It's a selection of people from different schools across the city." Rosie is a ballerina who wowed everyone earlier in the autumn with a dance number at the school's opening gala for the new Tsien Wing—the wing named after Gemma's family.

"Rosie Annabel Jones. That. Is. Amazing."

"It's not that big of a deal." She shrugs her shoulders, but the twinkle in her eyes tells me a different story.

"You've been chosen to represent the school. That's a huge deal." I give her a hug. "This calls for mango smooth-ies at lunch!" I'm so happy for her. She works and trains so hard. Just like Dev. I love seeing my friends do well. Hope-fully after today's field hockey end-of-season pizza party, I'll have some news of my own to share with Rosie and

Dev. I can already imagine the coach handing me the MVP award, and how my friends will be ecstatic for me when I tell them the news. I was even practicing accepting the award last night, until I was rudely interrupted by Millie.

"I humbly accept this MVP award for the Tai Tam Prep junior field hockey team," I said as I bowed to the mirror, placing a medal from a field hockey tournament in Ottawa over my head.

Then came a snort of laughter from behind me. "What are you doing? You're so weird," Millie said.

I slammed the bathroom door on her before throwing my old medal back in a drawer.

Millie's going to eat her words when I show her my MVP medal later today. I touch the spot on my chest where I imagine the medal will sit.

The junior girls' field hockey team meets in Mr. Chapman's classroom. He's an upper school PE/Wellness teacher as well as the coach for both the junior and senior girls' field hockey teams. He used to be a Black Stick, meaning he played for the New Zealand national team when he was younger—but that must have been a long time ago because his hair is all salt-and-pepper like Dad's.

I catch up with Saskia for the first time since our game.

"Cool drawings," I say, looking down at her sketchpad.

She's drawn a girl who looks a lot like her, even down to the ringlets and dark skin, wielding a flaming sword surrounded by planets and stars. "What's this from?"

"Thanks! I made her up—she's called Princess Esi." She flips through her notepad and shows me more intricate sketches of her warrior princess. I've never seen Saskia smile so widely before, not even when she scores a goal. "I want to be an animator at Disney or Pixar when I'm older. Maybe I can create a movie about her."

"That's amazing. Did you get to do that animation camp you mentioned?"

The huge smile on her face fades and she quickly shuts her notebook. "No, my parents wouldn't let me."

Before I can say anything else, Mr. Chapman walks in with the pizza. The smell of warm dough and tangy tomato sauce with oregano reaches my nose before he even opens the boxes. My stomach rumbles loudly, even though I had a big lunch, and I put my hand over it to cover up the sound.

"There's Margherita, pepperoni, and Hawaiian," he says as he cuts into the gooey cheese with a pizza cutter. "And there are some juice boxes in the cooler. No soda pop for real athletes," he says with a wink.

I grab a slice of Hawaiian, my favorite, but now that the pizza is on my plate, I don't feel like eating it. The butterflies in my stomach increase the longer we wait for the team awards to start. I'm definitely in the running for MVP. I had a great season and I scored that awesome reverse stick goal. There are other contenders too, besides me and Saskia—An Li Poulton is our goalie and let in only three goals all season and Scholastica Chang, our team captain, is our super sweeper on the back line.

Mr. Chapman must read my mind because he clears his throat and does the teacher clap—two slow claps followed by three fast ones, c l a p c l a p clap clap clap—to get our attention.

"You girls had a great season. Second in the league! And it was achieved through teamwork and grit. And now for the awards presentation you've all been waiting for—"

Mr. Chapman gives me a nod. "Holly-Mei Jones in her first season on the Tai Tam Prep junior team." The butterflies in my stomach disappear and I jump out of my chair to accept the medal he's holding out. I did it! I'm MVP!

"Congratulations on being our MIP," he says.

*MIP*? Did I hear that correctly? There is an awkward second as I stand there wanting to correct him—surely he means MVP. Is MIP even a thing? I'm confused and I'm glad no one can see my face as I bend my head down to receive the medal.

"Our most *improved* player," Mr. Chapman says as he

lays the medal over my head. "Great work with that reverse stick goal."

The blue, red, and white ribbon feels heavy around my neck. I feel so humiliated for thinking that I could be MVP. I look up and put on a smile and a forced cheeriness as I walk back to my desk, so the others can't tell that I was expecting a different award. Fortunately, attention quickly shifts away from me back to Mr. Chapman.

"And our MVP, most valuable player for the season is—" he pauses for a moment of suspense and does a pretend drumroll with his fingers on the desk. I look at An Li and Scholastica—they are both leaning forward with yearning.

"—Saskia Okoh. Great work on those penalty corners. No goalie in the city was able to stop those perfectly aimed shots. And the winner of the Hong Kong Golden Stick Award, no less."

I can't help but feel a twinge of disappointment. Yes, Saskia did score the most goals in the league. And she does train day in and day out. But what about those of us who try our best but who don't have private coaches and pushy parents? Are we less valuable? Forgettable?

I look over at her as she twists her dark brown ringlets around her index finger. She doesn't look surprised or even happy, even though she won the prize everyone else covets. We all clap and congratulate her.

After she receives her medal, Mr. Chapman drops another bombshell. "And Saskia did so well with the junior team, she will be joining the senior hockey girls' team next semester." She looks down at her shoes, avoiding looking at the rest of us.

A rush of words moves from my brain to my mouth and I can't swallow them before they escape into the open. "But she's only in Grade 7!" I blurt out. That's the rule. Grade 6s through 8s play for the junior team and Grade 9s and above play for the senior team.

Mr. Chapman nods along. "You are technically correct, Holly-Mei." He pauses. "But exceptions are made for exceptional players."

At this, Saskia's face reddens like the sauce on the pizza. And the way Mr. Chapman says *exceptional* makes it clear that he doesn't think I am. I shove slice after slice of pizza in my mouth to keep it occupied so I don't say anything else the rest of the party.

I leg it to the late bus and everything is a blur. Millie had better not laugh at me when she sees my MIP medal. Close to the exit, something black and white catches my eye—it's Jinsae's poster about the Grade 7 Inter-School Tri Tournament. Our team is set and officially entered. I can't help thinking about Rosie and her dance recital, and Dev and his elite hockey. I want to excel at something too. I may not have Saskia's invitation to play on the senior team, but maybe I can have this tournament. I know I'm supposed to be entering for fun. But what would be more fun than winning?

# 6

On Friday as I'm fixing myself an after-school snack, Millie bursts into the kitchen and pushes past me, opening all the cupboards.

"Are you looking for something?" Joy asks.

"I just want to see what we have, for inspiration."

"Inspiration for what?" I ask as I shut the doors left hanging open.

"The Lower School baking contest. It's run by Ms. Saarinen, the head of the Tai Tam Prep culinary club. We have to bake next weekend and bring it in the following Monday."

"What do you get if you win?"

"Oh, who knows? But I'm going to have fun creating my own recipe."

I open a pack of dried mangoes that Joy brought back from her Christmas visit to her family in the Philippines—she says her country's mangoes are the best and I have to agree. The sweet, but not sugary-sweet, taste sits on my tongue and makes everything brighter, happier, for a second. That is until Millie grabs the pack from me and shakes out all the slices into her hand.

"These would be amazing if we dipped half a slice in dark chocolate," Millie says as she rummages in the fridge for some of Dad's after-dinner chocolate stash.

However annoyed I am, that does sound delicious.

"There's another pack in the bottom drawer," Joy whispers to me with a wink.

An hour later, we flop on the sofa, full from eating Millie's mango-chocolate slices.

"Those were amazing—are you going to make them for the competition?"

"No, I don't think the younger kids will like the bitter dark chocolate. I was thinking something healthy but hidden inside something naturally sweet."

"Like zucchini cake?"

"Something like that. And it needs to be fun to look at on the outside."

The next morning, Millie and I try to convince Mom and Dad to let us go shopping on our own.

"We need to go to Wan Chai Market to get inspiration for Millie's winning cake recipe," I say.

"And I have to find a springform cake tin—we don't have one."

"Pleeaase?" Millie and I ask in unison, our arms linked in solidarity.

Mom and Dad look at each other out of habit—they might not have let us wander around downtown Toronto on our own, but Hong Kong is safe and they quickly agree. "As long as you make it for lunch on time," Dad says.

"On time," Mom repeats, tapping her watch face for emphasis. "Din Tai Fung only lets you sit when your whole group is there and you know how busy it is on weekends."

"No worries," I say. As if we'd be late for those delicious dumplings.

Since it's a bit windy out, I throw on my McGill University hoodie, a cozy present from Mom. That's where she and Dad met studying. I remember when I unwrapped it Christmas morning, Mom not-so-subtly said that *it's never too early to start planning for your future*. Even though she said she was joking, I was kind of annoyed at her for putting pressure on me at the time. I'm only twelve and three-quarters after all. But it makes me wonder what kinds of things Saskia's parents say to her about hockey.

Millie and I take the double-decker bus from the road

in front of our complex, Lofty Heights. We jostle to be first up the stairs, hoping the front seats are free.

"Bingo!" I say as I grab the window seat overlooking the sea, which also gives us a bird's-eye view of some of the fancy houses along Repulse Bay Road.

"I heard Jackie Chan owns one of these." Millie points at the mansions.

"I'm not sure about the gates though." I squint at the gaudy gold filigree fences enclosing some of the houses. It seems strange to have a golden gate—isn't that advertising you have lots of money and inviting thieves to check out inside?

We reach the peak of the hill and start going downward past the cricket pitch with its lush, rare-in-the-city real grass and the public tennis courts teeming with players. Happy Valley comes into view on the right. It's a valley between two peaks, with high-rises on either side. Dad says that Happy Valley is famous for the huge horse racing track, almost a mile around. My mouth opens wide every time I see what's in the middle of the track. Rugby fields, soccer fields, and not one, not two, but three field hockey pitches, including one that is Smurf-blue, like at school, which belongs to the Hong Kong Football Club. That's where Dev trains with the Hong Kong hockey team. He said I should try out for their youth squad—Saskia plays there too. But after the whole MIP vs MVP humiliation, I doubt if I could even make it. I hate that thinking about hockey, which I love so much, has started to give me a stomachache.

We get off the bus by the Sikh temple, with its gleaming white domes that look like upside-down flower bulbs. That's the temple where Dev and his family go for festivals and celebrations, like Diwali. There is a large Indian community in Hong Kong and Dev's family has been here for generations. I look at my phone and reread the text that Dev sent this morning. *I made the team for the Junior Asian Games!* he wrote. I sent him back a line of smiley face emojis. I'm so happy for him.

But now, thinking about it, my MIP award seems even more humiliating and heat rises to my face. I'm thankful when Millie pulls my arm to hurry me up, shaking these thoughts from my head.

We cross several streets and zigzag westward until we hit the outdoor market, marked by green stalls overflowing with plants and flowers, vegetables and fruit. An elderly lady with hair pulled back in a tight gray bun motions us over to her stall, saying "Siuje, siuje," *miss, miss,* and she offers us samples of a fruit already peeled and cut. I pop a juicy translucent piece into my mouth. It tastes a bit like a super sweet grape and it brings back memories of Ah-ma.

"Lychee?" I ask.

The lady shakes her head and points to a stack of red furry balls the size of eggs with wooden stems. They look like they should sprout legs and be featured on the *Muppet Show*. She says the name in Chinese and I shake my head, not quite understanding. She points to the black sign with the name in Chinese characters written in white chalk. I whip out my phone and open my Pleco dictionary app and draw the strokes.

"The Chinese name literally is *red-haired fruit*. It's a rambutan," I say.

The lady wraps our fruit in newspaper and puts it in the reusable shopping bag we brought. We quickly fill up on other fruit around the market like rose apples, which look like upside-down red roses, dragon fruit, a hot-pink-colored fruit the size of a tennis ball with green spikes, and a pomelo, a sweet grapefruit, but only one since Millie complains that it's too big and heavy to carry more.

I switch carrying the bag from one sore shoulder to the other as we make our way to Wan Chai Road and the aptly-named I Love Cake store, which is packed floor to ceiling with everything you might ever need for baking. Pans, mixers, molds, and specialty ingredients. Millie claps her hands with glee as she deftly moves between the cramped aisles. I hug the bag of fruit close to my body so I don't knock anything over.

"Should I get the round one or the square one?" she asks as she picks up and turns over a selection of baking tins.

"What about this heart-shaped one?" I pull it down from the top shelf.

"Oh! You are the best. I'm so glad you're taller than me. I didn't even see it." She does a little happy dance as she pays for the pan. "Will this fit in your bag?"

I sigh and take it, leaving her light on her feet as we head outside.

"Oh, the tram's coming. Let's hop on," I say. The tram is affectionately called the *ding ding* because of the sound the bell makes at every stop. It runs on tracks along Hong Kong Island and moves as slowly as you would expect a hundred-year-old double-decker tram to go. We sit on the top deck and Millie pulls out her phone and points it at the busy street scene below.

"Isn't it weird that so many roads in Hong Kong are still named after old British men? Do you think they'll change the names, like they did with Bombay to Mumbai or Peking to Beijing?"

"Geesh Hols, you always ask such boring questions. I

want to film this for my Insta stories—be quiet so your voice isn't in it."

"I wouldn't want to affect your number of likes," I say in a sarcastic tone. She's becoming increasingly obsessed with the reactions she gets to her posts.

"Whatever. You're just saying that because you never get any likes," she says.

"Um, that's because I never post." She knows I just like to scroll and observe.

After inspecting what she films, she uploads it and says, "I hope it gets lots of views."

She catches me rolling my eyes and she sticks her tongue out at me.

I guess I'll just have to ask Dad about the place names. He's a professor of Sino-British history and loves talking about old things. We snuggle on the sofa and watch documentaries together, especially when Mom is away working. Maybe that's why Millie is always tinkering in the kitchen, so she can avoid having to learn new things or risk being *boring*. She's totally missing out.

Millie pulls lip gloss out of her purse and puts it on using her phone as a mirror.

"Ah Millie, you know we're meeting Mom and Dad in about ten minutes." There's no way that Mom won't notice that hint of pink on her glossy lips. Mom says we're not allowed to wear makeup until we're *ready for university*. That rule is fine by me.

Millie has other ideas, though. "I'll just tell her it's Chap-Stick." Millie has a secret stash of makeup she buys with birthday money and she loves watching YouTube makeup tutorials. She flip-flops between wanting to be a chef or a makeup artist. She'll probably end up winning *The Great British Bake Off* or developing her own line of cosmetics. Maybe even both.

At the junction before Victoria Park (another British name, but she was the queen after all), we jump off the tram and step into the lobby of the restaurant. Mom and Dad are waiting with a numbered ticket.

Mom hands us each a menu with photos and descriptions of all the delectable dishes we can order.

"Mom, you already know what I like," I say as I pass her back the menu. I always get the same things. Why change it up when your favorites are so delicious? I join Millie at the window overlooking the dumpling-making station. There are a dozen people doing various tasks like kneading and shaping dough, scooping and weighing meat, and filling and closing the dumplings into perfect parcels, ready for us to order and savor.

Our number appears on the screen and we get seated at a round table and Mom passes the waitress the order sheet already filled out. Millie instructs us on the best ratio of soy sauce and vinegar to mix with the shredded ginger in our porcelain sauce dishes. After a few minutes, steaming bamboo baskets filled with xiao long bao arrive at the table. I reach over and with the white serving chopsticks, pick up two and put them in my bowl, before switching over to my black personal chopsticks. I like how there are rules for chopstick use, so we don't double dip. I hold the dumpling, filled with soup and a juicy meatball all wrapped in delicate dough, dip it in my sauce, and move to take a big bite.

"Be careful, Holly-Mei. It's going to be too hot," Dad says.

But I can't wait to eat it so I don't listen and take a huge bite of the dumpling. Searing pain fills my mouth. I feel like I just drank lava. I grab my glass of water and gulp it down to dull the pain, but it's only remotely helpful.

"Like this, girls," Mom says, as she holds the dumpling with her chopsticks and lets it hover over her porcelain spoon as she gently blows on it. Then after a few seconds she pops the whole thing in her mouth.

There isn't much talking as more baskets of steaming dumplings arrive, as well as plates of sauteed pea shoots, wontons tossed in chili sauce, and dandan mian, which are noodles in a spicy peanuty broth. Everything tastes good with a touch of peanut butter. But my tongue is still sore from my xiao long bao fiasco, and I'm constantly reminded of it every bite I take.

"So did you get what you need for your baking competition?" asks Dad.

Millie nods, her mouth full, and I say, "She's definitely a winner with her new heart-shaped pan."

"I don't care about winning. I just want to have fun in the kitchen and try new things out. And to see the great things all the other students make."

"Why join a competition if you aren't planning on winning it?" I ask.

"What happened to going out and having fun? Holly-Mei, I'm surprised at you." Dad puts down his chopsticks. He and Mom look at me expectantly, but I pick up another dumpling and start dipping it, my eyes fixed on my food, avoiding the question.

I'm a little surprised at myself for just blurting that out. I mean, I like winning, but what I like more is everyone going out and having a fair and fun competition. But since losing out to Saskia on MVP and being surrounded by such high-achieving friends, suddenly winning seems more important than it did just a few days ago.

# 7

I wait in the lobby of the Tsien Wing arts center auditorium, where the school held the opening gala exhibition that we worked on in groups last September. The wing is named after Gemma's family, who donated the funds for the new wing, and a larger-than-life oil painting of her grandfather presides over us like I imagine a painting of a monarch or president would. I sit in a leather armchair and pull out my flash cards. I spent the last few nights researching what to write on them. I await my team for the Dragon Dash—Rosie, Rhys, Gemma, Theo, Dev, Rainbow, and Snowy. One by one they trickle in and settle into the armchairs and sofas around me, but a few are still missing.

I look around for Dev but then remember he told me earlier that he has hockey practice.

"Where's Rainbow?" I ask.

"She can't come anymore—some last-minute eco-art meeting," says Snowy.

Not ideal, but I guess six out of eight present is not the end of the world.

"Thanks for meeting me. I'm so excited about our Dragon Dash team. I've never done an urban race before! I asked you all to meet up so we can have our first champion team boot camp."

"Boot camp?" Gemma asks, eyebrows raised. "I'm wearing my new Chanel ballet flats. I cannot possibly run around."

"Not that kind of boot camp," I say, laughing. "This is a brain boot camp."

I hear some loud groans, mainly coming from Rhys's direction. *What?* I mouth at him. "You said this would be fun. You're lucky I brought some snacks with me." He pulls out two Tetra Paks of chocolate Vitasoy and a giant bag of eel-flavored Calbee corn chips from his bag and starts munching.

"This will be fun, I promise." I point to the giant oil painting on the wall above us. "Who was he?"

I look at Gemma and put my finger to my lips so she doesn't divulge the information.

"Confucius?" Rhys laughs and bits of his corn chips go flying.

"Geez Rhys." Rosie puts her head in her hands. "You're so embarrassing."

"Guys, I know that's Gemma's grandfather in the painting, I'm just joking." Rhys turns to Gemma and says, "I know he was a famous businessman and philanthropist."

Gemma nods, satisfied that her family reputation is valued in this group.

"This is the kind of stuff we need to know for the Dragon Dash. I've prepared flash cards to help us study," I say.

"Before we get into that, we need to talk about something infinitely more important," Gemma announces.

I sit forward, waiting to see if she has a secret strategy or tactic to share.

"We need a team name," she says.

"That's the important thing you're talking about?" I try and raise one eyebrow like Mom can do, her silent way of asking a rhetorical *really?*

"Yes. Without a team name, I can't design the team uniform. Like I said before, winners need to look like winners."

"And I suppose you have some suggestions?" I ask already knowing the answer.

"Why, yes of course I do. Well, just one, but it's genius. The Gemstones. Get it? G-E-M like Gemma." She nods as she looks around at each of us. "We can get costumes with sequins and capes with embroidered stones. You know, like faux gemstones."

"They'll totally catch the sunlight on camera," Snowy says. She seems to be the only one excited about the idea.

"And we can upcycle them for Hallowe'en costumes," Gemma says. "I'm sure Rainbow would approve."

"How about something less sparkly? And maybe not named after you specifically since we are a team?" Theo smiles, his dimples on show, and that succeeds in melting any of her resistance.

We spend twenty minutes debating various team names, like Dragon Warriors, The 852s, named after the Hong Kong country code, and the Boba Babes—a suggestion that elicits raised eyebrows from the girls. We finally settle on Tai Tam Thunder. It's not super creative, but Gemma is happy she can use a thunderbolt as our icon on our matching outfits. And I'm happy we can get back to business.

"Okay, enough already guys. The Dragon Dash is less than three weeks away. We need to get up to speed on all things Hong Kong that might be asked of us. Ready, set, go!" I pull out my flash cards and start yelling out questions as if I were a game show host.

"Sorry, Holly-Mei, we need to head," Theo says as he and Rhys get up.

"But we've barely started the flash card round," I say.

"Rugby team meeting," Rhys says. "A champion team's work is never done. But I guess you wouldn't know that." He laughs and Theo and Rosie give him a hard stare. "What? I'm just joking. Don't be so sensitive," he says as he swings his backpack over his shoulder, knocking me slightly.

"Don't mind him, Holly-Mei. You continue—we're listening," Rosie says, nodding at me to start.

"Okay." I straighten my flash cards. "How much of Hong Kong is country park?"

"It's all concrete in the city, but there are so many hills and trails. I don't know, 20%?" Gemma says.

"I think more. Like 25%," Rosie says. I shake my head. "30%?"

"35%?" they ask.

"Clearly you guys have not been watching my YouTube channel closely enough." Snowy taps her satin bow ballet-flat-clad foot to emphasize her displeasure. "Forty percent of the land in Hong Kong is country park."

"Moving on: What does Hong Kong mean in Chinese?" I ask.

Rosie's hand shoots up. "Fragrant Harbour."

"Correct," I say. I'm about to move on, but Rosie continues, "Isn't that lovely? So romantic." Her eyes get all dreamy like they do right after she talks to Henry.

"What about Kowloon? What does it mean?" I say as I read the next flash card.

"Dragons," Gemma says. "Nine dragons, to be precise."

"On my YouTube channel, I talk about how it was named. Urban legend says that a young emperor noticed the eight hills by the sea and named the land *Eight Dragons*. One of his ministers reminded the emperor that he too was a dragon, so it was renamed *Nine Dragons*, Gau Long, Kowloon."

"Thank you, Snowy. That's exactly the kind of knowledge we need to stand out and win," I say, giving her a thumbs-up. "Sports trivia now: who won two silver medals in swimming at the Tokyo Olympics?"

"I know this!" Rosie's hand shoots up. "I met her at a meet and greet in Pacific Place. Siobhan Haughey! She was so nice. I even got to touch her medal."

"Good work guys. Next question: How many islands are there in Hong Kong?"

The girls start naming and counting them on their fingers—Hong Kong Island, Lantau, Lamma, Cheung Chau, Peng Chau.

"You guys aren't even close." I make a gesture to show there are more than the five they've mentioned. Many more. After a wasted couple of minutes of them discussing it between themselves, I blurt out, "You are so off. It's 263 islands."

I pull out my next flash card and I see people shifting in their seats and looking at their watches and phones.

"Phones down guys. We need to brush up on our knowledge. Okay, what's the population density of Hong Kong?"

"What does that mean?" Snowy asks.

"It means how many people live per square kilometer?" I say.

Nothing but blank faces look up at me. No one even throws out a guess.

"Come on guys. We need to memorize our facts. We're never going to win if we can't get simple things like this."

"I thought we signed up for a fun day out," Gemma says.

"It's totally going to be fun," I say in my most festive voice, then I ask more seriously, "But don't you want to try to win?"

"It's four o'clock. I need to run to make the late bus," says Snowy as she grabs her Hello Kitty knapsack.

"Guys, we need to work more," I say, pleading a little.

"You sound a little like Gemma did last September," Snowy says, referring to our gala project when Gemma made us stay after school every day to prepare. She was worried that her parents were going to send her to boarding school if she didn't do well. But we did a great job and her parents told her they might reconsider, which made her really happy.

"Please, even I wasn't this intense," Gemma says, as she packs her bag.

I stay seated in the armchair and sort through my flash cards.

"Aren't you coming to catch the bus?" Rosie asks.

"No, I'll catch the late late bus." There is another one at five thirty. Otherwise, I'd need to take public transportation home. I put my flash cards down gently on the table. They took me hours to make. "Rosie, do you really think I'm being intense?"

Rosie turns a delicate shade of pink. She does not like to say anything that might make others upset. "Well, we can tell this is really important to you."

"Why isn't it important to everyone?"

"You framed it as a day of fun. That's what we're all hoping to have." She smiles, leaving her unspoken message loud and clear, hanging in the air—*this will not be fun if you keep pushing*. I certainly don't want to potentially push my friends away. The word *fun* echoes in my head and gives me an idea.

"What about a fun day out with all the friends? Somewhere like Ocean Park?" I say.

"Oh that sounds brilliant. Could Henry come too?" Rosie asks.

"Of course."

"Oh goody! You should suggest it on the group chat."

I whip out my phone and draft a message: *Let's go to Ocean Park this Saturday. It'll be lots of fun.* What I don't say is that I have a plan brewing to get everyone to learn something while we are waiting in line for the rides. Everyone gets to prep for the Dragon Dash and no one will be bored standing around. It's a win-win situation. I press *send* and wait for the replies to come in.

In the meantime, I head to the Olympic-sized school pool to keep from staring at my phone. Luckily, I'm always prepared and have my swimsuit, cap, and goggles in my locker. And I'm glad to have some practice before the upcoming open water race. The chlorine smell is strong but familiar and strangely comforting—pools smell the same back in Canada. One side of the pool is filled with kids doing lessons. The middle few lanes are being used by the school swim team, who follow a random tune of whistles blown by the coach. The last two lanes are free for anyone to use. A big clock sits at the end of the pool— I'm not really sure what it does because it's not telling the time. It's like a giant plus sign and each arm is a different color. I'm afraid if I stare at it too long, I'll fall into a trance. At the end of the pool, every few seconds someone dives off the tower and does some flips and twists before landing with a soft splash. I put my goggles on and ease myself into the water and push off the side. As soon as I get moving, my head clears. I don't think about anything except the number of the lap I'm currently on. Nothing about how my friends bailed on my Dragon Dash brain boot camp or how I only have two weeks until the swim race. Nothing about needing to win. I feel lighter and freer than I have in ages.

# 8

On Saturday morning I meet Rosie and Rhys at their flat before catching the bus to Ocean Park together. I've been swimming after school every day this week and am happy to have a bit of a rest. Melody, their housekeeper, asks whether we want to bring any of her freshly baked brownies with us.

"Yes, please!" I follow her to the kitchen and sit on a stool at the counter as I fill up a plastic container with enough for everyone. I sneak a nibble of one and I drop some crumbs on my lap. When I pick up the crumbs and put them back in my mouth, I end up smearing chocolate on my new light khaki cargo pants that I got for Christmas—the only day I'm not wearing blue jeans or black leggings.

"Oh shoot." I rub the stain, but it keeps getting bigger.

"Would you like to go change? We can wait," Rosie says.

Rhys guffaws. "It's just chocolate, no one will notice."

I dab it with a wet paper towel and it seems to help. "No, it's okay, let's just go."

I put the container of brownies in my bag along with my hat and sunscreen. Mom insisted on me bringing the bottle so I could top up, even though it's January and the sun is not as intense as it was even just a few weeks ago.

"Rosie, are you wearing sunscreen?" I offer her mine.

"Yes, but only a low SPF. I'm hoping to keep up my tan."

Her fair skin glows with just the slightest hint of the sun's kiss left over from her trip to Thailand. I look at her fair complexion with a tinge of envy. Not because I don't like my olive-colored skin. Back home people say that I tan nicely from playing sports outside all the time, but since moving here, I've noticed that a tan is not something that is encouraged on Asian or mixed-Asian people like me. I see posters advertising whitening and brightening cream at every bus stop and subway station. I usually either tune it out or laugh about how silly it is, and then repeat to myself that beauty can come in all shades. But it is annoying to have that niggle in the back of my head when I'm out in the sun hiking or playing sports.

Rosie does a little pirouette. "Ready? I can't wait."

I can't wait either—a day of fun with my friends all together mixed in with some stealth brain boot camp.

"Let's go, already. I want to beat the lines for the Hair Raiser." Rhys says it's the best roller coaster ever. He pushes through us into the hallway and presses the down button multiple times as if it would make the elevator, or *lift* as they say here, come faster. And when we pile in, he presses the close button over and over again.

Once downstairs, we cross the street from the Lofty Heights complex just in time to see the bus go by.

"Oh no, we're going to be late," I say.

Rhys motions for us to follow him into a waiting red taxi instead. I never took taxis regularly back home, but it seems normal here, even to take them without an adult. When we get out a few minutes later, Rhys hands the driver thirty Hong Kong dollars, which is about the same price as a bubble tea, and he even gets change back.

We meet the others from the Dragon Dash team, plus Henry and Jinsae at the front gate. Everyone is excited about our day. There is already a crowd of people gathered, but we bought our tickets in advance so we can go in the fast queue. I'm so pleased with my brilliant idea to come here—now that we're in a fun place, my friends will be more open to practicing for the quiz. Instead of flash cards, I have a list of historical Hong Kong facts saved on my phone.

As we walk toward the central fountain, I pull out the blue-and-pink map of the theme park and start planning our route.

"Can we start by visiting the panda bears?" Rosie does a little skip.

"Of course, we can," Henry says as he leads us to the Giant Panda Adventure attraction. Rhys starts to object, but Henry shoots him a look and he goes quiet.

"I'll wait here. I don't want to see animals in captivity." Rainbow plops herself on a bench outside. "Even though in this case it's because their natural habitat is disappearing." I'm torn—she has a good point. But I've never seen a panda bear before, so I follow the others inside. The air is cooler than outside and it's a bit humid, like a greenhouse. In the first enclosure, I see the puff of black and white behind a hollow log—Le Le is sleeping. Or hiding. But in the next one, I see what looks like a giant stuffed toy come to life. Ying Ying, super fluffy and seemingly huggable, is munching on some bamboo, looking back at us, as if we were the ones locked up and on show. I can't believe that she's a real animal.

"She's so cute." Snowy points her camera at the panda.

She quickly changes her tone to something more serious. "I'm taking photos to help with Rainbow's eco-art project," she explains. Maybe she thought I was judging.

I have mixed feelings about seeing the pandas. I know that they can't be put back in the wild since they've been in the park for years, but they are so constrained. I wonder if anyone or anything could be happy under that kind of pressure, even if they are the star of the show.

After we're done with the pandas, we gather in the sunshine and I lead the group to the Old Hong Kong section. It's got a replica of an old city street with market stalls, dai pai dongs, which are open-air food stalls, and even a rickshaw. I'm thinking that maybe we can use them to learn something.

"Let's do a review of the different street foods." I pull out my phone and start taking photos of the menu for a pop quiz. Rhys has other ideas and he marches in the direction of the cable car station.

"We have to get to Hair Raiser before the queues start." *Queues* are what they call lines here. Everyone agrees with him and I don't want to seem intense again, so I put my phone away.

"I know you're really into this tournament," says Jinsae as we follow Rhys. "I forgot to tell you that the winner gets an interview and their team photo in the city newspaper's Youngspiration section."

I smile, thinking about how being featured in the city paper would be such a bonus to winning the overall tournament.

The cable cars are shaped like bubbles with fun purple, yellow, and red tops. The girls get in one car and the boys in the next one. Once we start moving, I check out the 360-degree view. At my back are the mountains that separate Central, the business district and all its skyscrapers, from the South Side. To my right, a sign in Chinese tells me the hill is called Nam Long Shan which translates to Southern Bright Mountain, or something like that. I'm super happy that I'm learning to recognize Chinese characters—we take Chinese in school for a period each day. It makes me appreciate the city more. I wonder how much easier reading characters would have been if I didn't insist on stopping Saturday Chinese school back in Toronto. Although I'm not going to tell Mom and Dad that—there's no way I want to hear them say the dreaded *I told you so*. I look to my left and there's a sheer drop down to the sea. Lofty Heights and Repulse Bay appear in the distance. Right below our cable car, I can see Deep Water Bay Beach and Middle Island.

"Look, swimmers." I point at the people outside the swim zone nets in the open water. That will be me and Rainbow next weekend.

"We're still on for our Tuesday swim, right?" Rainbow asks. We're meeting at Repulse Bay beach to do laps in the sea.

"Definitely." I wish Rainbow and I could have met earlier and more often to open water swim, but she's so busy with her eco-art stuff, it was hard to find a time that worked.

We meet the guys at the exit of the cable car and walk to the entrance of the Hair Raiser with its bright yellow tracks and red car. I've been on a roller coaster before, but not one that heads over a cliff like this one. Rainbow grabs my hand and before I can resist, she ushers me to the front row beside her. The car is floorless and my feet are dangling. My stomach is already aching with the thought of all the loop-de-loops. Theo and Dev jump into the front row with us. Rhys looks a bit disappointed not to have snagged a front-row seat but his face brightens when Gemma sits beside him. The worker pulls the safety harnesses over our shoulders and pushes them down tight. The silver gates open and our car starts to move up the first steep incline, right off the side of the mountain.

The cogs click slowly and I think, *This is pretty tame, what was Rhys making such a big deal about?* But then the cart gets progressively faster and louder as we move at an impossible angle upward. Theo and I look at each other with wide eyes as we reach the peak. All of Hong Kong South Side is before us for a split second before we zoom down into the first loop. We raise our arms in the air and scream through three more upside-down twists. Finally, the track levels out but I feel like we are going to go straight into the open ocean ahead. Right at the last second, the car turns toward land and we end back safe and sound, though I'm a little dizzy from the loops.

We exit the ride and Rhys announces he's going to go do it again.

"I want to sit at the front this time. Who's in?"

Snowy agrees to go with him so she can film it GoPro style.

"You too, Gems?" Rhys looks at her with wide puppy-dog eyes. She agrees and he looks ecstatic until she turns to Theo.

"There's room for one more in the front row."

"Nah, I'm good. My head is still spinning."

Rhys looks smug and as they walk away, I hear him claim something about how his head is completely fine.

We grab some smoothies and as everyone is sitting down in the sunshine, I pull out my Hong Kong fun facts.

"Okay guys, let's go over some stuff for the Dragon Dash," I say in my cheeriest voice. "What is the hole in the middle of buildings called, like at Lofty Heights?" I ask.

"Oh, it's for feng shui," Rosie says.

"Dragon, something," Henry says.

"That's it! It's the dragon gate," Rosie says as she flashes a smile to Henry, which he promptly returns.

"And who knows why it's there?" I ask.

"So that the dragon can flow freely from the water up the mountains." Theo starts speaking in a spooky whisper, "Legend has it, bad luck will befall any building that blocks the path of the dragon." The group oohs and ahs and starts talking about buildings in town that are said to be haunted, completely getting off track.

"Focus, guys." A smile is plastered on my face. "What is the date that Hong Kong was ceded to the British and who was the first governor?"

"Is that one point or two?" Dev asks, looking at Jinsae, who shrugs.

"I didn't have anything to do with designing the Dragon Dash course. I'm just the timekeeper."

"You guys should really know the date, so only one point," I say. China was forced to hand over Hong Kong to the British for 150 years until 1997. I've seen old photos of Hong Kong with the Union Jack flag and red postboxes and phone booths, but now there are red Chinese flags flying all over the city. We even have to sing the Chinese national anthem at school assemblies.

I try to perk things up and turn my Hong Kong fun facts session into one of me teaching them instead of me quizzing them.

"Did you know most apartment buildings don't have a fourth floor? Because the number four sounds like the word for death in Chinese."

"That's so easy. Everyone knows that," Rainbow says, slurping the remains of her smoothie.

"What about this?" Dev asks. "What year did the Peak Tram start running?" That's the famous funicular train that goes from Central up to Victoria Peak. Dev goes on to answer his own question. "1888. So many 8s."

"Because eight is a lucky number in Chinese culture." Henry chips in this tidbit. "Ba sounds like fa which means *to get rich*."

Everyone starts throwing in other facts.

"Did you know that Hong Kong is the city with the most skyscrapers in the world?" Rosie announces.

"Did you know that the best dumplings in Hong Kong are made by my maa maa?" Theo says proudly about his grandmother's cooking. Everyone starts laughing. My friends seem to be having fun and are learning at the same time. I feel a warm glow in my chest.

Gemma comes and finds us after their second turn on the roller coaster, squeezing into the space between me and Theo on the bench. "What's so funny—why is everyone laughing? What did I miss?" She looks around, eyes wide and demanding.

"Nothing, Theo is just showing off about his grandmother again," Dev says and he gives me a wink. Theo and Dev had some history last year about a science project, but they are back to being close friends again. I would like to think it's thanks—at least a little bit—to my intervention last autumn.

"Hey, my maa maa is a superhero in the kitchen. It's not only her dumplings—you guys should come over and taste her sticky rice pudding cakes when she makes them for Chinese New Year." Theo's grandmother lives with them. I feel a sudden twinge of sadness thinking about spending Chinese New Year without my own grandmother. Ah-ma and I used to make decorations out of red paper and put them all over the house, even on the front door, inviting fortune and luck inside. I hope luck still visits us this year, even though she won't be around.

We spend an action-packed morning running around

doing the other rides—the pirate ship, the giant swings, the carousel. We even visit the aquarium with the giant jellyfish and shark tank, which of course Rainbow skipped, but she did say that at least the sharks were saved from being hunted for their fins. Rainbow really does walk the talk—when she was in Grade 5, she started a petition at school to ask the luxury hotel chain owners, whose kids go to Tai Tam Prep, to stop serving shark fin soup at their banquets, and they did! Even a ten-year-old with a vision can make a huge difference.

We finally pause for a lunch of burgers and chocolate milkshakes.

"Spill some already?" Gemma asks in front of everyone with a smirk, pointing at the brownie stain on my pants from earlier. I see her flash a look to Theo as if seeking his approval, but his face is blank. No dimples on show, thankfully.

"No, just a messy eater." I laugh at myself to show her I genuinely don't care that she just tried to embarrass me. "I totally forgot I had these. Who wants one of Melody's brownies?" I say as I pull out the plastic container. I pass it around and everyone takes one. When I get the container back, it's empty.

"Here, we can share." Dev breaks his in two and gives me half along with his huge megawatt smile.

"Thanks!" I say.

"You can have half of mine too," Theo says, offering me a piece, dimples on show.

I shake my head. "I'm good, thanks."

"Then I'll have it, Theo." Gemma eagerly takes his piece and pops it in her mouth. I bite my lip to keep from laughing.

For the last ride of the day, we head to the Raging River flume ride. It's a gentle ride along a pretend stream, until we get to the end where we swoosh down to the bottom of a steep hill, all of us getting splashed in the process.

"Good thing we did that one last, I'd hate to walk around wet all day. My pants are soaked. I've been sitting in a puddle."

Gemma looks at me with her eyes wide and then whispers something to Dev. He quickly unzips his hoodie and passes it to her.

"Tie this around your waist," Gemma says, handing it to me. "Quick!"

I want to protest but something about the alarmed look on Gemma's face makes me do as she says.

"You didn't sit in a puddle. You got your period," she whispers into my ear.

Heat rises up from my neck to my face until I feel like my head is on fire. I'm completely mortified. Who else besides

Gemma noticed? Dev must know, otherwise he wouldn't have given me his hoodie. I look at him but he is avoiding my gaze. I whip my head around to look at Theo—he and Rainbow are laughing. Are they laughing at me?

"We'll be back in a second." Gemma takes my hand and I follow her in a daze. She pulls me into the nearest bathroom. I look at the back of my pants in the mirror and see a dark red stain peeking out between my legs and I want to cry.

"Do you think anyone else noticed?" My voice is squeaky.

"I don't know." She shrugs. "But don't worry, it's not a big deal."

"I'm so embarrassed. I don't have a pad or change of clothes with me."

Gemma opens her Gucci backpack and pulls out a pink quilted pouch and passes me a pad.

"I always carry a little emergency pack for when this happens," she says.

"Mine isn't regular yet. I usually get it every six to eight weeks, so I wasn't expecting it today."

"I learned the hard way with an accident last summer. I was wearing white shorts. My mother was so embarrassed, but you know what? It happens. It's natural. As I said, it's not a big deal."

"Thanks for helping me. Saving me." I can't but wonder

why she's being so nice, especially since she could have completely embarrassed me in front of everyone, especially Theo.

As if she could read my mind, she says, "Look, Holly-Mei. I will make fun of you for some things, but never something like this. Us girls need to stick together."

Without thinking, I pull her into a hug. She's as surprised as I am, but she accepts it and squeezes my shoulder before stepping back.

"Oh look, you can wear these." She pulls out a pair of black leggings from her bag. "I brought them to wear under my skirt in case I get cold, but I'll be fine. You take them."

"Are you sure?" I ask and Gemma nods. "Thanks again for helping me." She made the choice not to embarass me. And even though I don't really understand why she was so kind, I'm still super grateful.

## 9

Even though the rest of the day at Ocean Park was fun and no one said anything about my period accident, I wake up the next morning with a heavy feeling in my stomach—not cramps, but like it's full of rock-shaped portions of doubt. Joy helped me wash my khakis and Dev's hoodie, which I fold up and put in my school bag, along with a pack of raspberry Twizzlers to give to him at school tomorrow—it's his favorite candy, mine too—as a thank-you for saving me from embarrassment.

Or should I even feel embarrassed? Mom said a period is natural and accidents happen and not to worry about it. She ordered me some special period underwear online, which she said she wished they had when she was my age because she had accidents too. She also told me if people are uncomfortable, they should be the ones who are embarrassed that they can't deal with nature. But who knows how people are going to react when they hear about this at school. Are they going to judge me? Think I'm a loser? I better get their minds onto something else so they forget about my period.

Something like winning a big inter-school tournament.

The morning is perfect for running. It's cool, but warm in the sunshine, and not humid at all. Thank goodness there's no more sauna-level heat and humidity for a few more months. I head down, cross the street, and start stretching in the beach parking lot. I look up at Lofty Heights and at the giant square hole, the dragon gate, in our building. I imagine the dragon flying from the sea through the hole up to the mountain behind. I love learning new cultural things about the city. Dad promised to take us to the Hong Kong Heritage Museum up in Sha Tin today, but we had to postpone because Millie is at Lizzie Lo's extended sleepover birthday party all day.

I run along the boardwalk to Deep Water Bay Beach. There are sailboats moored in the channel to Middle Island, where there is a yacht club and small pier. I guess that is where we will do the relay handover on race day. In front of me, the Ocean Park gondola bubbles move back and forth along the peninsula. In the large bay, there are yachts and junks anchoring for the day. The traditional meaning of *junk* is the red-sailed old wooden boats you see on Hong Kong postcards; Dad told me the English name comes from the old Portuguese word jonco. But nowadays, *junk* usually means a party boat. Millie was on one yesterday for day one of Lizzie's two-day twelfth birthday bonanza. I reach the end of the boardwalk and stop to admire the view before running back the way I came.

A girl with a ponytail of dark curly hair whooshes by me. It's Saskia—I recognize her long stride and pink scrunchie. I pick up my pace and run behind her all the way back to Repulse Bay. There's no way I'm going to let her outpace me. Thankfully, she stops at the beach parking lot—I am shattered from keeping up with her. Her mom is there waiting for her, tapping her watch. And she looks annoyed. I stop and pretend to tie my shoe so I can listen.

"Saskia, that was almost a minute slower than last time," she says. "What's wrong with you this morning?"

"I'm just tired, Mom."

"Fine." Her mom's tone softens but is still matter-of-fact. "But on race day, you need to push through."

"And I'm hungry, too."

"I have some fruit in my bag. Or what about ice cream? There's that new gelato place everyone is talking about."

I get up and try to walk away unseen but Saskia notices me. "Oh hey, Holly-Mei. Were you just running?"

"Yes, I'm training for the tournament."

"Saskia is too," her mother says. She turns to her daughter and says, "Now that you know you have stiff competition from Holly-Mei here," Mrs. Okoh winks at me, "you better improve your time." I can't tell if her mother is being serious or not. "Would you like to join us for ice cream? My treat," she asks.

"Sure, thanks, Mrs. Okoh."

"Just call me Eleanor."

"Okay, Mrs. Okoh." I cannot call a parent by their first name—it would feel too weird. Plus, Mom and Ah-ma would be mortified by my lack of manners.

We head to the new gelato stand, Vincenzo's Gelateria. There are a lot of people standing on the beachfront plaza licking their cones, faces turned to the sun like flowers. A young Chinese woman asks us what we would like. Saskia's mother asks about the different flavors, whether any are lactose-free, and if they have gluten-free cones. She orders a raspberry sorbet and Saskia and I both get chocolate mint chip gelato which turns out to be both our favorite flavor. Maybe I'll find out we have even more in common. Even though I'm still envious of her being asked to play for the senior hockey team, there's no question she's an excellent field hockey player. She's a head taller than me so her reach is wide and she is the fastest runner on the team. Plus, she works hard for it. Harder than I ever have. Can I complain about not getting glory if I don't train as hard?

Just as I'm about to ask her if she wants to go for an open water swim this week after school, her mother starts speaking again to the server loudly and in an exaggerated slowness as if it will make the order more clear. "I want it in a cup, not a cone. C u p." She makes a charade gesture with her hands for cup, even though I don't think she actually specified that she wanted a cup when she ordered.

"Gosh, you would think the level of English here would be better. I mean, isn't this a former British colony?" Saskia's mother laughs and looks at us as if expecting us to laugh with her. But Saskia just looks down at her feet, embarrassed. Or I hope she's embarrassed. I stare at Saskia, openmouthed, waiting for her to call her mother out. But she doesn't. I want to say something, but the words get caught in my throat. *She's someone's mom*. Mom and Dad have always said to respect our elders, so I don't know if I can say something. I thought adults were supposed to be the ones who behave well and teach us by example. But this is one example I don't want to follow. I thank Saskia's mom for the cone and lick my gelato quickly, so I don't need to spend any more time with them than I need to. In fact, I'm more determined than ever to beat Saskia in this tournament.

After dinner, Millie finally comes home from Lizzie's sleepover party. Millie and Henry's sister have become inseparable since the autumn. They've bonded over their love of baking and both have secret stashes of makeup which they try on but remove before any adults see. Millie throws her bag in the front hall, kicks her shoes off, and flops down on the living room sofa where I'm sitting with Dad and Mom watching a David Attenborough documentary about penguins.

"Oh my God, Hols, we had so much fun. Did you see my stories and posts? Yesterday, we took the junk up to Sai Kung to this beach that you can only get to by boat. It was like our own private tropical island. And today, Lizzie's mom surprised us all with a visit to the spa at the Peninsula Hotel. See my nails!" She flashes her ruby-red nails in the air and wiggles her fingers. I notice Mom cringe. She doesn't like us wearing any nail polish, especially a bright color.

"I wish you would have chosen something more neutral," Mom mumbles.

Dad laughs and says, "Gracie, it was a birthday party. A special occasion, it's okay just this once." He kisses Mom's hand.

"And I had a massage! I fell asleep it was so relaxing." Millie laughs so hard she snorts. I feel a little twinge at her fun day at the fanciest hotel in town—I've never been to a real spa before.

"Wow, sounds like a very nice party, poppet. Have you eaten? Would you like some dinner?"

"No, I'm stuffed." She pats her stomach for emphasis. "After the spa, we had high tea in the lobby. There were these teeny tiny sandwiches." She makes small rectangle shapes with her hands in case we can't imagine how teeny tiny they were. "Cucumber sandwiches are surprisingly good. I thought they would be totally boring. But the coronation chicken—what is up with that? Raisins!" She makes a face and sticks her tongue out. "But the scones and pastries were so good."

"Speaking of pastries, darling, isn't your baking competition this week?" asks Mom.

"Shoot! It's tomorrow. I was having so much fun, I totally forgot." Millie laughs and slaps herself on the head. "I'd better get baking."

"I'll help," I say. I've seen the penguin program before and plus Millie might have a stress meltdown.

In the kitchen, she rummages through the fridge. "Double shoot."

"What's wrong?"

"We're out of butter. I'll have to run downstairs to the grocery store."

She's only gone for a few seconds before she comes back. "It's closed already." She shrugs. "I'll just replace the butter with something else." She scans the kitchen cupboards and says "Ah-ha. These soft avocados will be perfect."

"Avocados? Instead of butter? Won't that mess up your recipe?" Ah-ma says recipes are like rules—best to follow them.

"Nah, I'll figure it out and make it up as I go along. Plus, it'll have cocoa in it. Everything tastes better with chocolate."

I can't believe how relaxed she's being about this. "But won't this ruin your chances of winning the competition?"

She shrugs. "I just want to participate, you know, create something yummy. As long as it's delicious, I don't care if I win."

I look at Millie and don't know what to think. But I'm going to be here to support her when she's all upset because she lost.

# 10

Monday afternoon, the email on my laptop pings with the daily school bulletin. When I open it, there is Millie's smiling face next to her triple-layered heart-shaped chocolate avocado cake. The headline is Amelia-Tian Jones wins the Lower School Baking Contest with the subheading Secretly Healthy "Heart of Chocolate" Creation Steals the Show. The first paragraph goes on to say how Millie hopes to be the next junior Masterchef or winner of *The Great British Bake Off*, junior edition.

Snowy calls from a few rows back, "Holly-Mei, do you think I can interview your sister for my YouTube channel?"

"Sure, I guess."

"Think she can share that recipe with my sister?" asks Henry. "That cake looks delish."

Even Gemma chimes in with "Wow, your little sister is kind of cool. Who knew?" I can't tell if that's genuine surprise that someone in Grade 6 could be cool or whether it's a dig directed at me, as in "who knew unexceptional, period-leaking Holly-Mei Jones could have a cool sister." Because it's Gemma, I tend to focus on the latter.

The day passes achingly slowly. Although Millie is in a different wing, I still feel her presence in the chatter throughout the day. Even Theo and Dev ask me if Millie could save a piece of her winning cake for them to try. I lie and say that it's all gone. I don't know why I lied or why I wasn't happier for her. Maybe it's because I know winning isn't important to her. She barely tried for the competition—she was too busy getting a massage and manicure to be bothered to be prepared with all the ingredients, let alone remember the competition was even taking place. And then she goes and wins it. It's not fair.

I deliberately skip the regular bus home. I don't want to hear any more gushing about Millie and her cake. I want to go swimming and clear my head in the water, but I still have my period. Mom bought me some tampons, but I haven't dared to use them yet. I have so many questions and I want to sit with her and get some answers before I try them. So, instead I run along the Tai Tam Country Park Trail home. It's a flat path with forest on one side and the Tai Tam Reservoir on the other.

By the time I get to Repulse Bay, my head is clear. I'm soothed by the view of the water and hills as I walk the last bit along the beach. The sun is starting to set and the westward sky is turning a fiery orange with a hint of neon pink. I forget all about Millie until I get home and find Dad at the dining table digging into a giant slice of her prize-winning cake.

"Oh poppet, have you had any of this cake? Come and try." He holds a fork up and I reluctantly take a bite. It's good. More than good. It's super delicious.

Dad looks at me expectantly.

"It's okay. Not bad," I lie.

"Not bad? It's absolutely divine. Your sister has a real knack for baking, don't you think?"

I shrug. Dad doesn't press me more—he's too busy eating the cake. "Good thing your mother has a work event until late tonight, otherwise she'd be annoyed that I'm filling up on cake before dinner." He continues eating, even picking up the crumbs and licking his fingers.

Millie is in her room, lying on her stomach on the bed, scrolling her phone. The phone she's not even supposed to have until she turns twelve, like I had to wait, but she whined until my parents caved in. "Look Hols, my cake win post has over two hundred likes! It's a new record."

"So, you *do* care about winning." My tone is accusatory.

"I didn't, but now that I've won, I'm happy I did." She shrugs nonchalantly, which annoys me even more. She flashes me her phone. "Check out my story." The video zooms in on the judge's face, Ms. Saarinen, trying her cake and relishing every bite. Then it moves to a photo of the cake with the first prize ribbon next to it. And ends with a selfie video of Millie saying, "Future winner of a TV bake-off right here." She flicks her dark wavy hair, flashes a v sign with her fingers, and laughs with her trademark snort.

I wait until 7:00 p.m. on the dot to FaceTime Ah-ma.

She's an early riser and this is the best time to call her before she does her tai chi.

"Baobei, zaoshang hao." *Good morning, my treasure.*

"Hey Ah-ma," I say and lean back into a stack of pillows on my bed, their softness cushioning my bruised ego.

"I hear Amelia-Tian won baking competition. Good girl."

Ugh. Is that the only thing anyone can talk about?

"Sure, yes it's great for her." Then I mumble, "Everything's always so great for her."

"Holly-Mei, that sounding sour."

That's Ah-ma's code for anything that seems petty—*sour*. I don't care. I feel like I just ate a box of Sour Patch Kids, extreme edition.

"It's not fair."

"What is not fair?" she asks.

"Millie didn't even try. She just threw something together last minute and she won."

"But she has talent in the kitchen."

I ignore the remark and continue. "She claims she didn't even care about winning. But now she's posting it all over Instagram."

"Is this really about your sister?" Ah-ma gives me a quizzical look. "But you not even liking baking," Ah-ma says gently.

"I'm not only talking about baking. I'm talking about

Rosie and her selection for the cross-city dance performance. Dev and his Hong Kong U14 hockey squad. Even Rhys and the rugby team won their championship. And the worst one is Saskia—she not only got the Golden Stick *and* MVP, but she got asked to play for the senior team, even though she's only in Grade 7. It's not fair."

"Not fair to you?" Ah-ma asks, sounding a bit confused.

"I'm tired of people winning everything and getting all the glory. I try so hard, but I feel like no one sees and I get left behind."

"Ah baobei. Sometimes people having talents that you cannot match, no matter how hard you practice. There is a saying, 自知之明 zi zhi zhi ming, *knowledge of oneself*, meaning you need recognize one's own strengths and weaknesses."

"What, and just accept that I'm not exceptional?" My mind flows back to Mr. Chapman talking about Saskia. *Exceptions are made for exceptional players.*

"If everybody exceptional, then word has no meaning. You have to accept you have limitations. Everyone does. And everyone has own strengths. You will find yours. Real friends do not care whether you win a trophy. Stop focus on winning, on glory. And work to be the best friend you can be."

But someone always wins—why can't it be me for once?

I don't want to argue with Ah-ma because I don't want her to start listing out my limitations. I just smile and change the subject. Normally talking to Ah-ma makes me feel better, but today, she doesn't make any sense at all.

# 11

Today we have early dismissal from school for some sort of teacher-training workshop, so Rainbow and I head to the beach to take advantage of the noonday sunshine and start open water training. I'm a confident swimmer, but there's something about the ocean, the salty water, and the wind that makes this more daunting.

"Nice swimsuit." Rainbow eyes my new black racer-back one-piece decorated with bright yellow lemons.

"My mom just ordered it for me. It's for when, you know—" I lean in and whisper "—you have your period."

She motions for me to twirl around so she can see the back. "Cool," she says as she nods approvingly.

Rainbow opens a mesh bag and pulls out a wetsuit. "This should fit you. It's my old one—I had to get a larger one since I started growing taller." Rainbow was my height when we started school last August, but she has shot up almost half a head since then.

Somehow slipping on a wetsuit makes this endeavor more serious. I put my feet through the legs and gently pull the tight rubbery-smelling suit up, gentle pinch by gentle pinch until it's sitting at my waist.

"You look professional already," says Rainbow with a smile. She must sense my nervousness because she adds, "Don't worry."

I put my arms in the sleeves and tug until the suit fits over my shoulders. Rainbow grabs the string attached to the zipper and does up the back, finishing with a light tap on the Velcro fastener at the neck.

"Did you get those earplugs I recommended?"

I show her the bright orange silicone pieces in the round plastic case. She said they're to keep the cold water out.

"Great. Roll one between your fingers and pop it into your ear." I follow her lead and soon I feel like I'm wearing earmuffs because she's talking but I can barely hear her. She gestures to our orange inflatable swimming buoys, which click on around our waists. We are swimming within the shark net, but Mom and Dad insisted that I still wear one, which is fine as I feel more comfortable with it on anyway. Rainbow already calmed my concerns about the term *shark net*. Apparently, there are no sharks, but she said the net keeps out other things. I didn't dare ask what the other things are.

I dip my toes into the water. It's not as cold as I expected. The big digital clock on the beach shows the time and the temperature. It's 20C/68F both outside and inside the water and the breeze has calmed. Rainbow gives me a countdown on her fingers, 3—2—1 go! And we run into the sea and dive in. I follow her lead and swim behind her all along the net as we head to the other side of the crescent beach. I feel like I am swimming harder than I do in the pool, but am moving slower, like the small waves hitting my face are pushing me backward. Every time I come up for a breath, I make sure I can see her orange buoy ahead of me. The few strokes that I didn't, I found myself veering off to one side. It's hard to go straight when you don't have lines like the ones on the bottom of the pool to follow. After what feels like an hour, we arrive at the other end of the beach. I lift up my goggles and pull out my earplugs.

Rainbow clicks her stopwatch. "Okay, that was about fifteen minutes for 500 meters. Decent time. But think you can pick up the pace on the way back?"

We were only swimming for fifteen minutes? "Are you sure your watch is correct?" I ask like I'm joking but I'm totally serious. I got a sports watch for Christmas but I haven't started using it yet. I still like my old analog watch which isn't waterproof—it was Ah-gong's, my late grandfather's, old Timex. Its light brown leather strap is old and weathered, but soft and smooth, which reminds me of Ah-gong's face.

I let out a deep breath. "Yes, sure, pick up the pace, no problem."

"The trick is to keep your body constantly moving side to side and reach as far as you can with your arm on every stroke." She reaches her arm out to show me. "That's what gives you your forward momentum."

I follow Rainbow, elongating my arm reach like she said as we loop back along the net toward the part of the beach we started from. By the time we're almost done, my head isn't just clear, it's empty, just like my legs are empty of energy, and I can't think of anything except the shoreline coming closer and closer into view. Relief washes over me when I can finally feel the ground. I push myself forward and after a few lunges, make it out onto the beach.

"What?" I ask when I see Rainbow's lips move. She points to my ears. Ah, the earplugs.

I take them out and the background starts to hum like normal.

"So, how was it? Different from the pool, right?"

"Exhausting. But exhilarating."

"Good to hear. You can decide whether you want to do the first leg to Middle Island or the second leg to the finish line at Deep Water Bay. It's about one and a half times what we did today. It should take you about forty-five minutes, max."

I'm feeling confident. I'm tired, but with more practice and tips from Rainbow, I'm going to be ready. I have just a few days until the race.

We move away from the sand and take our wetsuits off in the outdoor shower by the plaza.

"Want to come over? We can make up a schedule for training before the race."

"I'd love to, but I can't today, I have to meet with my eco-art club. We're planning an art installation for the Chinese New Year Fair and we're heading to Sham Shui Po to get supplies."

"Okay, do you want to meet and swim again tomorrow after school?"

"Um, I'm meeting my eco-art group again."

"What about Thursday?"

"I'm at an art workshop. We're going to design a mural for a rejuvenated playground. What about Friday after school? I'm free then."

That's the day before the race. I can't believe she's not

more keen to practice. Why is she prioritizing her eco-art group over training for this tournament? No pain, no gain, right? But I don't want to push her away—I can't do this race without her. "Sure, Friday. Can I use the wetsuit during the week? I'm going to swim again."

"Of course you can. You sure are taking this tournament seriously."

I want to say, *Like you should be*, but instead I say, "It'll be more fun if we do well, right?" It's a question but it comes out sounding more pointed than I intended. I know I shouldn't have said it in that tone and I smile to soften the aftereffect.

Rainbow doesn't say anything for a second, as if she's looking for the right words. "I told you that I'd only do this for fun, that I have my eco-art project," she says, eyes focused on the mesh bag as she stuffs her wetsuit inside.

"Yes, of course. I'm only joking. I'm just really happy we're doing this together," I say.

"Okay, I'm glad we're on the same page," Rainbow says, in a tone reminiscent of my mother.

Instead of going home, I head over to Rosie's in the next tower. I need to have one of our cousin popcorn-and-sofa sessions, or I'm going to burst. I can't wait to taste that sweet and salty popcorn we always make. Her doorbell chimes like Big Ben and the tune gets stuck in my head.

Melody opens the door and I apologize as I take my shoes off and realize I've traipsed in some sand from the beach.

"Rosie is in the kitchen, popping popcorn," Melody says.

"Great. She must have had a sixth sense that I was coming," I say as I skip toward the kitchen.

But when I push open the kitchen door, it's not only Rosie at the stove but Henry too.

"Hi! So glad you're here. We're taking a break from our Battle of the Books training and we've made much too much popcorn." Rosie opens the lid and gleaming puffs overflow from the pot. Rosie and Henry have been on the school Battle of the Books team for the last two years and have started recording book reviews for Snowy's YouTube channel.

Henry laughs and picks the kernels off the stovetop and puts them in a big ceramic bowl. He shakes some salt over the bowl and I take a spoonful of sugar and make to sprinkle it over the warm popcorn. But Henry grabs the bowl and moves it out of the way, so my sugar spills all over the counter.

"What are you doing with that?" Henry asks, looking aghast.

"What I always do—put sugar on top. It makes it taste like kettle corn."

"No way are you putting sugar on my popcorn!" Henry laughs. I frown. This is how Rosie and I always do it.

Rosie, ever the peacemaker, brings out a second bowl and splits the batch. "Holly-Mei, put yours here and sprinkle salt and sugar on it. Henry, you use this bowl."

"Great idea, Rosie." He flashes her a smile, and the light off the stovetop bulb reflects off his braces, making him look like his teeth are twinkling. She has a matching twinkle in her eyes. *Yuck.*

We gather on the sofa and start chatting. Rosie asks about my swim and I just give her a monosyllabic answer. I don't want to get into Rainbow and her lack of drive and desire to win in front of Henry. This is cousin-to-cousin private stuff.

"I meant to tell you. I know you love the Shang-Chi film. They're playing it again at the cinema in Causeway Bay on the weekend."

"Oh, I love that movie. Xialing is the best, so strong and cool. I'm definitely up for going. Last time I saw it, Mom was gushing about Shang-Chi's dad the whole time and it was really annoying." I laugh as I remember my mother giggling about the actor Tony Leung, wondering aloud if she'd ever bump into him in Hong Kong. It hasn't happened yet, but Mom says she still holds out hope.

"We're planning on seeing the five o'clock show. Are you in?" Henry asks.

I am about to blurt out, "What, you're coming too?" but I bite my lip to stop the words from coming out. So, Henry is not only getting in the way of my kettle corn, my Rosie sofa session, but now our movie night? Things have changed so quickly since they started hanging out. What if they start dating and Henry becomes *her boyfriend*? Will things change even more?

# 12

The day of the swim relay race has arrived. I sit down at the table to see that Dad has made a batch of his fluffy pancakes with extra bacon.

"I even made some maple butter," he says as he dabs a spoonful onto the stack on my plate.

They taste sweet and wonderful, but I can't eat more than a couple of bites.

"I'm too nervous to eat. Plus, I don't want to have a stomach cramp," I say.

"You'll need the energy, honey." Mom puts down her newspaper and places her hand over mine. "It's a long swim. Are you sure you are up for it?"

I'm not really worried about the length. I know I can swim the distance, but will I be fast enough? This is the first of three events, followed by the Dragon Dash and the trail run. And all the times are cumulative, so every second counts. "Completely. Ready to win."

My parents look at me with raised eyebrows. Before they can say, *it should be about participating* or *winning isn't everything*, I add, "Just joking," to preempt them.

Mom, Dad, and Millie come with me to the edge of the beach to find Rainbow. I spot her outside of the temple in front of the giant statue of Tin Hau, the goddess of the sea. She is said to protect sailors, fishermen, and hopefully swimmers. The statue's white robes appear to be flowing and the patterns of the gold tiles glint in the sunshine, making her seem alive, ready to look out for us.

Rainbow already has her goggles around her neck and wetsuit on her legs with the top half hanging at the waist—she looks like she could be in one of those triathlon magazines. I suddenly feel like a complete amateur as I change into my borrowed wetsuit. How did I even think I could compete with the other kids? Many of them have raced before, either in the sea or on a school swim team. Rainbow needs to help me to pull the wetsuit on when it gets stuck on my legs—my hands are trembling too much. She zips me up and whispers into my ear, "It's okay. You've got this." I exhale deeply and try to push all my worries out of my body.

I pass our bags containing dry clothes and flip-flops to my parents.

"We'll meet you girls at the finish line." Dad dabs some sunscreen onto his neck.

"You've got your safety buoys, right?" Mom asks. We flash her our bright orange buoys that are attached to our waists. We even blow them up in front of her so she can relax a bit. "And there's a boat bringing up the rear, right?"

"Don't worry, Mrs. Li-Jones, there's a boat at the back as well as the front and on both sides of the swim pack," Rainbow says matter-of-factly, putting my mother at ease.

"Okay, off you go then girls," she says, giving us each a hug. "Oh wait." She grabs the sunscreen tube from Dad and dabs some on my nose "to protect from the sun." She might as well have said *prevent you from tanning*. I push her hand away as she says, "What? It's waterproof."

"Rainbow, would you like some?" Mom asks.

"It's okay. My mom made me put some on before I left." Rainbow gives me a knowing smile. As we start to walk away, she says in a low voice, "She doesn't let me leave the house without it—she says the sun brings out my freckles."

"Your freckles are super cute," I say. Rainbow shrugs.

I wonder if all Asian moms are the same when it comes to the sun and worries about tanning. Mom is wearing a sunhat and most of the ladies at the beach are equally covered. Some even have those welder-like visors on.

I hear Millie yell, "Hey Hols," and we turn back to look in her direction. "Don't swim into any jellyfish!" She laughs at my openmouthed reaction and I hear Mom and Dad getting annoyed at her. They wave and blow me kisses and continue heading toward the boardwalk as if some scary bombshell wasn't just dropped onto my lap.

"Rainbow! What was she saying about jellyfish?" I grab her arm to stop her from walking.

"Oh, I wouldn't worry about it. It's not jellyfish season," she says. "There might be some since we're swimming outside the nets. But it's winter so there won't be very many."

"They're not like the ones we saw at the Ocean Park aquarium, right?" I ask, picturing those big, *no*, giant, phosphorescent creatures with a hundred tentacles, ready to slap and sting me.

"No, they'll be small, but you should be able to see them and move out of their way. Plus they won't sting too much."

*Too much.* My mind reels. Rainbow must sense my worries because she touches my arm gently. "You're in a full wetsuit. You'll be fine." I nod as if I believe her because I want to believe her. *Need* to believe her.

The beach pier is heaving with swimmers ready to race. There must be a hundred of us. We walk toward the registration desk where we sign in and get our race swim caps. Bright pink, so easy to see in the water, and they have our team number printed on them with big black waterproof marker. Apparently, they were going to give us disposable race bibs, but Rainbow convinced Jinsae to ask the organizers to give us reusable swim caps instead. The lady at the desk tells us the second relay swimmer needs to go to the pier now and take one of the shuttles to Middle Island.

"Okay, this is it. I'll do the first leg, right?" she asks.

Initially, I wanted to do the second leg because I was imagining the glory of being the first one out of the water and the cheers I'd get from the crowd. But I know that Rainbow is a stronger and faster swimmer than me and it would be more strategic to have her finish because she's more likely able to make up time.

"Can you go second? I think it'll help us get a better time."

"Are you sure?"

"Yes, we'll do better with you at the tail."

"Okay, let's do it!" She smiles confidently and gives me a high five.

I walk her to the edge of the pier with the other relay swimmers waiting for the shuttle boat. I see Saskia in line and we nod civilly to each other. We haven't spoken since that day with the gelato. I wonder if she was embarrassed.

I'm thankful that I won't be swimming the same leg as her—I don't want to run into her mother again. Although I wonder who her relay partner is. Rainbow and I hug and wish each other good luck before she steps onto the boat.

Now that Rainbow is gone and I'm all alone, I'm not nervous anymore. I'm *petrified*. I follow the other pink-capped swimmers toward the beach like I'm on autopilot. In the roped-off starting enclosure, I copy the others and do some windmill arm and side stretches before adjusting the goggles on my face with my shaking hands. Then a booming voice on a megaphone starts counting down from ten. The air crackles with excitement and I start breathing too quickly, my head starting to spin. Then I remember to breathe in and out super slowly to calm myself down, like Ah-ma used to tell me to do when I would hyperventilate.

When the horn goes off, I move with the crowd across the sand. As soon as my feet touch the cold water, I snap to attention and adrenaline flows through my body. I know what to do. I've trained for this. I dive in and start swimming as fast as I can. After a few minutes, we hit the net that encloses the part of the beach that is patrolled by lifeguards. The net that filters out sea animals, like big fish. And apparently jellyfish. I push myself over it and suddenly feel like I'm in a totally new environment, even though it's the same water I was just in. But wilder.

I block out all thoughts and concentrate on the neon pink heads bobbing up and down in front of me. I push myself forward, faster than I've ever swum. I make my way through the crowd. I get past someone on my left and I feel an arm nudge my side, but I continue forward. A person swims past me, too closely, and I get a kick on my shoulder. That fuels my adrenaline more and I want to catch up to the kicker, so I push harder, even though I cannot tell who they are anymore in the sea of pink caps.

As we leave Repulse Bay behind and head into the narrow channel beside Middle Island, the pink bobs in front of me grow fewer and fewer, until there is just a handful left. I stay close behind the person in front of me—Dad said it's better to swim in someone's wake because there is less drag. I'm not exactly sure what that is, but it sounds like it will slow me down. I see the second-leg racers on the Middle Island beach coming up to my left and I'm relieved that I only need to push myself for a few more minutes. I've got this, no problem. I concentrate on having long strokes, efficient breathing, powerful kicks. I'm going to be so fast that Rainbow won't need to make up time to catch up and come in first.

But why can't I be first for this leg? There's no reason I can't do this. I ignore Dad's advice and pull out from behind the person in front of me and rush forward full tilt.

I don't see any more pink heads between me and the beach and a thrill passes through me. That feeling stays with me for a second until I feel something on my face. A bunch of fine threads, like a spiderweb. I brush it off in a panic, but it gets tangled in my fingers. I shake my arm vigorously until the strands disappear. Slowly, a stinging sensation spreads across my face and onto my hand. My breaths become rapid and I suck in some water. I start coughing and even more salty water splashes into my mouth. Some of it comes from the splashes of the swimmers passing me.

I've lost my slim lead and now there are bobbing pink heads in front of me. I realize that I'm not moving, just treading water. I need to get going again, but I'm too scared to put my face back in the water. What if there are more jellyfish?

But then I see Rainbow on the beach, with the unique bright turquoise stripe down her wetsuit, waving her arms at me, mouthing something. I can't hear her, even though she's cupping her hands. She looks like she's cheering me on, encouraging me. I take a deep breath, close my eyes, and put my head down, forcing myself to move my arms and legs until I feel the sand under my feet.

The official clocks my number and gives Rainbow the go-ahead to jump into the water. She will need to swim hard to break free from the middle of the pack. I feel like I've let her down. I shouldn't have gotten ahead of myself like that. If I was paying closer attention, I could have avoided the jellyfish. Instead, I swam into something that was right in front of me.

Once Rainbow is out of sight, I sit on the sand and drink the water someone has handed to me. I pour some down my face to ease the stinging, but it only makes it throb more, before eventually subsiding. After twenty minutes, the organizers round up the first-leg swimmers. I toss my water bottle in the recycle bin and I board the shuttle boat that will take us to the boat club at Deep Water Bay Beach and the finish line.

All the swimmers are gathered by the food table where the boat club has put out a strange combination of cut-up fruit, cheese sandwiches, and spring rolls. I spy Rainbow eating some pineapple chunks.

"Hey!" I'm afraid to ask how we did in case she gets annoyed at my jellyfish panic attack. But I needn't have worried. She greets me with a big hug.

"We came in third!" Rainbow beams.

"Really? Even after I blew my lead?"

"Was that you? I saw someone start to panic right near the beach." Her face is full of concern. "What happened?"

"Jellyfish!" I put my head in my hands as I recall the silky filaments. "It felt light, like a spiderweb on my face. Then it stung."

Her eyes widen. "Was it bad? Does it still hurt?"

"It's okay. It lasted a few minutes. I think the thought of it was worse. But I don't want to be in the water when it's actually jellyfish season." I shake my head. No way.

"A team from the Canadian school won. And Saskia's team came in second. She was partnered with Lindsay Liang—she's on the Tai Tam Prep swim team."

I feel petty for being happy she didn't come first and I console myself with a handful of spring rolls.

Mom, Dad, and Millie wave from the other side of the club deck. As I walk toward them, I pass Saskia and her mother in a heated conversation that I can't help but overhear.

"Only second place?" Saskia's mother asks.

"Mom, second place out of fifty teams is good," Saskia says defiantly.

"Why do you think I wanted you paired with Lindsay from the swim team? So you could win, that's why. Your father won't be pleased either." Mrs. Okoh shakes her head.

"Mom—" Saskia takes a deep breath. "It's just one race."

"It's not just a race. How will you expect to make the Olympics if you can't even win a school competition? You need to excel at everything if you want to achieve your Olympic dream."

"It's not *my* dream. It's *your* dream. And you had your chance but you didn't make it." She stares squarely at her mother before buckling and looking down at her feet.

"That's enough. We're leaving." Her mother turns and stomps off toward the road.

I stand there like a statue in case they see me. I don't want them to know I heard something so personal. I watch Saskia follow her mother, shoulders hunched. It seems like the weight of all Saskia's awards are heavier than the medals themselves.

# 13

At school on Monday, we get an extra-long lunch hour so we can start planning for the Chinese New Year Flower Fair. It's a full-day event held the day before we break for the holiday and get another two weeks off school. Mom was complaining that we were just off for Christmas and wondering when we are going to learn anything at school if we're always off, but Dad gently reminded her that Chinese New Year is the biggest and most important holiday in Hong Kong.

The Flower Fair is planned and run by the Upper School kids and the fun is mainly for the Lower School kids. But the Upper School kids can come in during breaks and lunch hour. Students get to play games and shop for candy, Chinese-zodiac-themed toys, and of course, flowers. Ah-ma and I used to buy flowers together right before the New Year celebrations—she said they represented growth and good fortune after a long winter.

The older grades organize the ordering of stuff to sell, while the Grade 8s are in charge of decorating, and the Grade 9s are in charge of the photo booth. The Grade 7s get the best job though—planning the game stations.

I'm heading to the library to meet the others when I hear my name.

"Hols, wait up." It's Millie running down the hall. She grabs my arm and stops to catch her breath. "Guess what? I've been asked to make my baking-contest-winning cake for the Chinese New Year Flower Fair. The PTA wants to showcase what's been going on in school for some important visitors."

"Oh. That's great for you." I push my shoulders back to keep from slumping and try not to sound as flat as I feel. Millie is still reaping the glory from her win, even though she won without trying. She told me she's gained a ton of followers since then, with her daily culinary creations getting more and more likes every day. I try to block out Ah-ma's voice telling me about Millie's "talent in the kitchen" or the fact that other people might have skills I can't match, no matter how hard I practice. Instead, I focus on something she just said. "'Important visitors'? Like who?"

"I dunno. Something about school donors."

School donors, like all the important business people who were at the Tsien Wing opening gala last September. People that Mom had said were in a different sphere. If these people are going to be at the Flower Fair, surely the PTA will want the winner of the Inter-School Tri Tournament to be on hand too. Images of Millie and me together at the fair, her with her heart-shaped cake and me holding a giant trophy, flash through my head.

"Earth to Holly-Mei." Millie waves her hands in front of my face. The images in my head melt like snowflakes landing in my warm hand. "What do you think?"

"About what?"

"Didn't you hear anything? I was asking if you wanted to bake something and put it on my stand. I'm going to make mini versions of my winning cake and sell them at the Flower Fair. I bet I can make enough money to buy one of those special ring lights."

"Ring light?"

"You know, the ones that make you look good on camera. They take away shadows and make your eyes sparkle."

"As interesting as a new lightbulb sounds, I am too busy training to think about baking."

"Suit yourself. But don't ask to borrow my light for your stories or posts." She turns on her heel and walks away. I notice people, Upper School students that I don't even know, say hi to her. Someone even says, "Your Insta story was hilarious." Her giggles reverberate down the hall and straight into the pit of my stomach.

When I get to the library, I take a seat at a table where Rosie, Gemma, and Snowy are already sitting. They're drawing up a list of potential games for the fair, but I can't concentrate. My mind keeps wandering to images of me with a trophy being interviewed by the city paper, of Millie and me as the stars of the Flower Fair.

I'm quickly drawn back to reality when I hear the word *prizes*.

"What kind of prizes are there for the winners?" I ask.

"Everybody gets some sort of prize," Snowy says.

"There are no winners?" I ask.

Gemma raises her eyebrows at me. "Some of these kids are five and six years old. Everyone is a winner. Everyone gets a candy."

I raise my eyebrows back at her to show my displeasure at the questionable life lesson we are teaching these little kids. That sounds like everyone at a tournament getting a participation medal so no one gets upset they didn't win.

By the time we have to head back to class, we have a

list of games that the little kids will surely love, which I wouldn't mind playing myself: pin the tail on the dragon; the chopstick game, where kids move mini marshmallows from bowl to bowl; and a wind-up animal race with the twelve animals of the Chinese zodiac. All with prizes donated by Gemma's family—I just found out that they not only have a toy manufacturing empire, but a candy factory too.

"Let's meet after school for a bit. We still need to organize a couple of games for the older students," Rosie says. The whole table agrees. I'm a bit annoyed that everyone is so keen to plan the Flower Fair, but no one has been available to meet with me for more Dragon Dash brain boot camp since our visit to Ocean Park. At least we'll get together later today. It will be the ideal time to whip out my flash cards. The Dragon Dash is this coming weekend and after our third-place finish in the swim relay, I can almost taste victory.

At the trill of the dismissal bell, I head to my locker to pick up my flash cards and other goodies that I found in Dad's study. He has a collection of books with all these black-and-white photographs of Hong Kong in the olden days. They show busy market scenes, old white men in suits being carried in something called a sedan chair by Chinese men, and young women in white shirts and black pants with their hair in one long shiny braid that almost touches their knees. I wonder how they felt about foreigners taking over their land and telling them where they could and couldn't live. Dad told me that in the olden days, the Chinese weren't allowed to live on the Peak, the nicest area in town.

I meet up with my friends back in the cafeteria. Rhys, Jinsae, and Theo each come with a plate full of steaming dumplings.

"What?" Theo asks when he sees our openmouthed faces. "Rugby just started up again."

"We need to fuel up. Or be fodder," Jinsae says as he blows on his plate to cool the dumplings down.

"Good one, mate," Rhys says. "Want one?" He offers a dumpling to Gemma, who politely shakes her head. Then Rhys pops it into his mouth, whole. His eyes go wide. "H-h-hot inside." He jumps up and runs to get a glass of water.

"That's it," says Snowy. "We need to have a dumpling eating contest!"

"Oh, that is going to be so messy," Rosie says with a giggle, her hand covering her mouth.

"That's why it'll be great on video." Snowy makes a pretend zoom lens and focuses in on Rhys. "Your brother can be our poster boy."

"You don't have to participate if you don't want to," I say, sensing that was Rosie's worry. Her eyes always go wide whenever I drop something and still eat it under the "five-second rule" so I don't think a dumpling-eating contest would be her kind of fun. Rosie smiles with relief.

Rhys is quickly roped into doing a demo video as he gulps down his remaining dumplings, which have now cooled. The others throw around other ideas for games.

"What about a Tai Tam Prep karaoke contest?" Henry asks. Rosie had told me that Henry has a really nice voice. He even brought his guitar over to her place and sang when they were on a study break.

"Nah, silly idea," I say. I don't want to encourage him to spend any more time practicing with her. They're always together as it is.

"What about a dance-off to K-pop music?" Jinsae asks.

"This is for the Chinese New Year Fair. Shouldn't it be Chinese music?" I blurt out. I mean it's right there in the name of the festival.

"Actually, it's the Lunar New Year. Celebrated by all the countries that go by the lunar calendar," Jinsae says proudly. "Like Korea. We call it Seollal. And in Vietnam, it's called Tet."

I feel my face heat up. Sometimes I forget to think before I open my mouth. But Jinsae doesn't seem offended—he looks happy that he was able to teach us something about his culture. And he looks even happier when Rainbow says, "A dance-off sounds like so much fun. You can be the first to sign up and show off your moves."

I think more about what Jinsae said. There are lots of students of Korean and Vietnamese heritage at school. "Should we change the name of the festival to include all the cultures that celebrate the Lunar New Year?" I ask. "We could call it the Lunar New Year Flower Fair."

Everyone nods their head enthusiastically. "Fantastic idea, Holly-Mei," says Theo.

Gemma chimes in. "I can talk to Ms. Nguyen about it and drum up support in the school paper."

I feel great that my idea has everyone excited. And it wasn't even about winning something, just about being thoughtful to others. I reach inside my bag but then hesitate. It doesn't seem like the best time to pull out my flash cards. Everyone is having fun and laughing and chatting. I decide not to spoil the mood and risk being seen as intense again. I can study all the materials by myself, so at least I'll be able to answer the questions on behalf of the team.

Something bright and shiny catches my eye from across the cafeteria. It's a bunch of Grade 8 kids with samples of potential decorations for the festival. I hear one say that they are all in storage in the school basement, so they can reuse and upcycle everything they need. Rainbow would be happy to hear that. Everything they pull out of the box is red, trimmed with brilliant gold. Colors that bring in good luck for the new year. Then I see what caught my eye—a whirling windmill. The spinning motion of the red, green, and golden blades is hypnotic.

I pick one up and blow on it so it spins. Snowy steps beside me and takes a photo.

"The light hit you perfectly," she says as she checks the image. "Did you have these back in Canada?"

"Yes. My grandmother and I would make homemade ones. To spin away the bad luck and bring in good luck for the New Year."

"My po po takes me every year for a haircut, to cut away the bad luck." Snowy snaps another photo of me. "Anything else you do with your grandmother?"

Lots of things, I think. I help her make dumplings and noodles to feast on. She gives Millie and me each a new Chinese dress to wear for our special New Year's Eve dinner. "Mahjong," I say. "We'd play after dinner with our parents, but she would always stand behind me and Millie, guiding our hands." Making sure we did okay and didn't make any silly mistakes. I wish she were here to give me some guidance right now.

# 14

It's a beautiful, sunny, cloudless day and the rugby pitch at Tai Tam Prep is heaving with students ready to start the Dragon Dash—fifty teams of eight from schools all over the city. Our team gathers in our matching black shirts with golden, sparkly thunderbolts across the front and black satin superhero capes with blue-and-white sequin trim, a nod to the Tai Tam Prep colors. I spy Saskia and her team, The Miss Fits, in neon tank tops and matching headbands, standing by the goalposts. Mr. Kelly, the school rugby coach, stands on a makeshift stage at one end of the field and welcomes everybody. He explains the rules of the day: we all need to download the Dragon Dash app, which is where we'll get clues and answer questions; we can only use public transportation (no taxis); and only our team members, identified with our green wrist-bands, are allowed to participate. The race is organized so that the tasks are done in random order, so not all of the teams head to the same station at the same time. "And remember, no googling the answers! That would defeat all the fun. But you can use the maps app to get around. And for all the finishers, there will be a barbecue at the West Kowloon Waterfront Park this evening." We all cheer loudly.

"Goody, a party. Do you think Henry can join in, even though he's not on the team?" Rosie asks. I don't know why I find this really annoying, but I do.

Luckily Rhys chips in with an answer. "You heard Coach Kelly. Only team members."

"That's too bad. We wouldn't want to break the rules and get disqualified," I say.

Rosie shrugs and looks a little disappointed but is quickly diverted when a ping goes off on all our phones.

"Guys, time to concentrate, the first clue has dropped," I say, rallying the team. I start the timer on my new sports watch so I know exactly how long we're taking.

We rush together to a secluded end of the rugby pitch so our discussions won't be overheard by any competing teams.

*By the ancient village of Chak Chue, the pirate Cheung Po Tsai might hang and ask "WhatSUP?"*

What is this? A riddle? My stomach drops. No one said anything about riddles. And nothing about this was in the material I studied. I've never even heard of Chak Chue. I check with the others—none of them have either.

"Theo, your family has been in the Hong Kong shipping business for more than a hundred years. Do you know anything about pirates?" I ask, grasping for straws.

"Guys, forget about the pirate. Look how the last word is written," Rainbow says. "WhatSUP with upper-case SUP." She points at the letters on her phone. "That must mean something."

"Like SUP, stand-up paddleboard?" I ask.

"That's it!" Theo says. "The pirate—isn't there an old pirate cave in Stanley?"

"Theo, you're a genius," Gemma says grabbing his arm, her eyelashes fluttering as she looks at him. "Chak Chue means *Bandit's Post*. It's the original name for Chek Chue, the Chinese name for Stanley."

"Stanley Main Beach," Snowy says, "has a water-sport rental place. They must have SUP boards."

We all high-five each other and make a mad dash up the road to the nearest minibus stop. We see another team with a moose and maple leaf on their T-shirts—they must be from the Canadian school—running up the hill behind us but luckily after we get on the minibus, all the seats are taken and the driver won't let them on. They will need to wait another few minutes for the next bus, giving us a smooth lead. I look out the back window and see another team at the bus stop. Competition is tight.

When we reach Stanley Beach Road, Snowy yells, "Yau lok mm goi," and the driver stops. We all say "mm goi" as we get off, which is that magic word I was taught when I first arrived, which means *please, thank you,* and *excuse me,* all rolled into one.

We rush to the sandy beach and look around for any signs of what to do.

"What are we looking for?" Rhys asks.

"Clues. Someone dressed up as a dragon?" I put my sunglasses on—the sun is reflecting off the water into my eyes.

"Look!" Rosie says. "There's a person dressed up as a pirate."

I turn to where she's pointing. "Great work, Rosie!" The pirate is under a beach umbrella and looks just like a regular sunbather, except for the eye patch, striped shirt, and tricorn hat.

We rush over to him and Theo says, "Joh-sun," *good morning*. "What's up?"

A very long second passes. In that time, I see the people on the beach—families with little kids—stare at our satin-caped group. We must be a funny sight.

The pirate doesn't say anything but hands Theo a piece of paper—it's a voucher for an SUP rental with a map of the beach buoys printed on the back.

"It's a course. We need to paddle around the buoys and back, right?" Dev looks at the pirate. He nods.

"Great," I say. "Who's done this before and wants to volunteer. Someone who will be fast and not fall off. Every second counts." I tap the Dragon Dash app on my phone for emphasis.

Gemma volunteers, "I'll do it. I've done yoga on SUP boards so my balance is pretty good."

"Are you fast?" I blurt out.

She shoots me a look. "I know this is a race, Holly-Mei. Yes, I'm fast."

I feel bad for doubting her in front of everyone. Then she says, "Besides, if I fall in, Theo can save me, isn't that right?"

"Sure, no problem, Gems," he says, giving her a gentle punch in the arm and they both start laughing.

"Holly-Mei, Gemma's got this. You have to chill," Rhys

says. The others nod. I've learned enough to hold my tongue and just go with it. It's only the first stop in the race—I don't want to come off too intense at the start of a long day.

And Rhys was right. Gemma is a natural on the board—she glides effortlessly between and around the buoys like she's done it a hundred times before. The thunderbolt on her top shimmers in the sunlight, and her cape flutters, making her look like a real superhero. We yell and cheer from the beach. When she jumps off the SUP and hands the paddle back to the guy at the rental place, he gives her a code which we put into the app.

A green checkmark appears on all our phones and we give each other high fives.

"How do I check the team standings?" I ask.

"Is that important?" Gemma asks. I can tell by her tone that she's testing me to see how much I care what position our team is in.

"Of course not." I smile and put my phone away. But as soon as she turns her head, I find the leaderboard on the app. We are first. Yes!

With a ping, our next clue drops.

*Man oh Man, I wish to do well on my Lit exam.*

Another riddle that is completely out of the reach of my

flash cards. Why didn't I put riddles in my boot camp? I'm sure Dad would know how to unravel this, but asking him would definitely be against the rules.

"Let's walk to the bus terminus while we think, so we'll be ready once we know where we're going," Rainbow says.

"Literature exam? Do we need to go back to the school?" Gemma asks.

"That seems a bit random," Rhys says.

"What about the word 'wish'?" I ask. "That must be important."

"There's a wishing tree! I go there with my family every Chinese New Year. You need to write what you're wishing for on a piece of paper, then throw it into the tree. If it stays, your wish will come true. If it falls, it means your wish was too greedy," Snowy says.

"Fantastic," Rainbow says. "Where is it?"

"Lam Tsuen, up in the New Territories," she says.

"Yikes, so far. It's going to take us ages to get there," Rainbow says.

"What about a temple? I read that lots of students go to temples to wish and pray for success on exams. Is there a temple that is famous for this?" Rosie asks.

"That's it!" I say, finally happy to be able to share some

knowledge. *Man, oh Man.* I think it's Man Mo Temple! It's in Sheung Wan, right beside Central."

We all do a little jump for joy. And thanks to Rainbow's foresight, we're already at the bus stop when the bright yellow double-decker bus arrives. It takes us into the city in less than thirty minutes. We get off downtown and start zigzagging our way up through busy streets lined with restaurants and shops until we reach a set of steps.

"Come on, the temple is at the top." Dev takes the steps two at a time, his cape billowing in the breeze. When we reach him, we are facing an old temple dating back to the 1800s, its single story dwarfed by the high-rises built around it. The cylindrical green roof tiles look like they are made of jade coins and there are intricately carved drag-ons, flowers, and miniature people all along the ridge. We step inside the front gate, which is flanked by two pillars and some railings carved to look like bamboo, and into the courtyard of the temple.

"What now?" asks Rhys.

"How do you make your wish here? Is there a wishing tree?" Rosie asks.

"Actually, you bang on the temple drum to ask for your wish to be granted," I say.

We step past the granite guardian lion and into the main temple in search of the drum. Despite the interior being painted red and bright gold, it is dark inside. Dozens of conical-shaped incense coils with red tags containing prayers hang from the ceiling giving off swirling smoke as they burn.

"I don't think it's in here," Rhys says in a loud voice.

Theo nudges him and gives him a shush. "We're in a temple." I like how even though we're in a race, Theo still thinks about being respectful.

"I think it'll be close to the entrance," Gemma says. "You say your prayer inside, then bang the drum before you leave."

Snowy spots it in the corner. "You go for it, Holly-Mei," she says. "I'll film you banging the drum."

"Are you sure, guys? It was a group effort," I say. Everyone agrees and I feel a burst of pride as the others encourage me. My perfect plan of getting everyone together is officially working—we just need to work a bit harder on the winning part. I take the thick wooden stick and bang the drum. *Boom* it goes, with a low deep rumble. I look up expectantly, waiting for something to happen, some indication that our group was right about the clue. But nothing happens. Did I lead the group to the wrong place? What if Snowy was right and we're supposed to be at the wishing tree? We all look at each other and shrug.

Then we hear it, the click click click of a zoom lens camera from the person standing next to us. He looks like someone dressed up as a tourist for Hallowe'en, complete with a button-down shirt in a bright flower pattern, shorts, white socks and Velcro sandals, and a Hong Kong guidebook in his hands. He opens up his book to reveal a blank page with a code, which we tap into our Dragon Dash app. A green checkmark appears along with our next clue. We're tied for first on the leaderboard with a team from the American school, the Starz n' Stripes. Sweet. Let's keep this up.

We spend an exhausting day running around the city on buses, trams, and the metro, even taking a cable car up to the Big Buddha statue. After every stop, I check the board. When we got to Lantau, we heard one team was so desperate to win, they used one of their drivers to chauffeur them between stations. Now they're disqualified. The Tai Tam Thunder are consistently in the top five. As long as we stay here, I'll be happy.

Thankfully we are at our final event, at the Museum of Hong Kong History, the museum we visited last September when we saw Theo's family's photos and that famous family heirloom necklace. My watch beeps—it's six o'clock, the sun has set, and we are hungry. We have been eating our homemade snacks on the run, but our energy is running low. We are doing a quiz-off with a team from the British school, the Licorice All-Sorts, dressed in matching T-shirts with the image of pastel-and-black candy on the front, which is making my mouth water. It's a quiz on Hong Kong history. This is a sure win. After four questions, we are tied.

"Last question," the quizmaster tells us. "And the tie-breaker."

We lean forward to make sure we can all hear clearly. "The last Governor of Hong Kong before handover, Chris Patten—"

Okay, I've flipped through his biography in Dad's office. I've got this.

"What was his favorite dessert and what shop was it from?"

What? I should have known after all the riddles we've had to solve today that our last question would be something I couldn't read in a book. I look to the others—they seem excited. This is a good sign. We huddle over our answer sheet. "Egg tarts," Snowy says softly. "There's a large framed photo of him eating dan tat in the shop." Everyone nods in agreement.

"Great," I say. "What's the name of the shop?"

"I know it. It's on Lyndhurst Terrace," Rosie says.

"Right on the corner of Hollywood Road," Dev says.

"I know the one. I agree—their egg tarts are the best, especially when you get them warm and the pastry is at its flakiest," Theo says.

"That's all fine, but what's the name of the shop?" I ask. There are lots of shrugs.

"Ten seconds left," announces the quizmaster.

"Come on, guys, think!" I say with force as if it will force the answer to pop into their heads.

The whistle goes and I reluctantly turn in our sheet with only half the answer.

"You both have the correct answer of 'egg tarts' but only one team got the name of the bakery correct, 'Tai Cheong'." The quizmaster looks to the other team. "The winner of this round is the Licorice All-Sorts from the British International School. Congratulations and well done to both teams."

Both teams get the green checkmark for completing our task, but the other team gets extra points for winning the quiz. I frantically reload the leaderboard on my phone to look at the stats. There must be a mistake—I don't even see our name amongst the top five teams anymore. I refresh and refresh again, the rainbow-colored pinwheel turns and turns, but the outcome is always the same. We have dropped off the leaderboard and have finished in sixth place. All this effort for nothing.

Rosie touches my arm gently. "Holly-Mei, are you okay?"

I realize I'm gripping my phone so tightly, my knuckles are white. "It's fine," I say. But it's not fine. I can't pretend anymore. They are all smiling and laughing, like losing doesn't matter. "Guys, we blew it. We aren't even in the top five."

"How did we do?" Dev asks.

"We came in sixth place," I say.

"That's great, though. Isn't it? Sixth out of fifty sounds pretty good to me," Snowy says.

"We were top of the standings after the first event. We should have had that answer. I should have run more boot camps. All that effort's been wasted," I say.

"Wasted? Don't be silly. Didn't you have fun? Didn't we see lots of amazing places? Kai Tak Cruise Terminal, the Big Buddha, Kowloon Park." Rosie puts her arm around me and gives my shoulder a little squeeze.

"I guess so." I sigh and let out a deep exhale.

"So then, isn't that the most important thing? That we had fun together?" she asks.

I look back at my phone and stare at the leaderboard. The team from the American school, the Starz n' Stripes, won the Dragon Dash. But I wonder if they had fun. When we crossed paths with them at the metro station earlier in the day, it sure didn't look like they were enjoying themselves. There they were, eight kids in red, white, and blue top hats, arguing over whose fault it was that they lost precious time when they missed their stop and had to turn back.

"Come on, Holly-Mei. You have to admit that it was a great day," Dev says.

"And a huge thanks to you for organizing," Theo says.

I seem to be the only one feeling disappointed we didn't do better. Maybe I should take a cue from them and chill about this winning stuff. Now that I think of it, it was a great day. My plan was always about getting the gang together to connect and have fun, and we did that. It shouldn't have been about winning. I look at all their smiling faces and can't help but smile myself. I feel a release in my chest, like I was holding my breath, but didn't know it.

"Thanks, guys. Now, come on, we have a barbecue to get to!" I say and we head down the steps, our satin capes flowing, toward the twinkling lights of Kowloon.

# 15

Back at school on Monday, still basking in the glow of the fun we had on the Dragon Dash, I pop by Coach Chappie's office. I want to ask about field hockey summer camps. When I arrive, Saskia's already there. She looks up and smiles when she sees me, and I smile in return.

Coach Chappie hands her some papers and says, "Your parents need to sign both forms to allow you to play on the senior team. We have to get special permission from the league since it's an exception."

She nods and tucks the papers in her doodle-covered notebook and waves goodbye to me.

"Good morning, Holly-Mei. What can I do for you?" he asks.

I'm still thinking about Saskia's papers—the ones that

let her play on the Tai Tam Prep senior team, even though she's only in Grade 7. Coach's comments from the pizza party and the MVP mess ring in my head: *Exceptions are made for exceptional players.*

"Um, I forget. I'll come again later," I say as I back out of his office and run down the hall. I turn into the stairwell and dash up a couple flights of stairs before stopping. As I lean against a random locker to catch my breath, something becomes more clear than ever—I have to beat Saskia in this tournament.

The next and final event is this coming weekend— the race along the Eight Immortals Trail. Even though we came in sixth place in the Dragon Dash, because we finished third in the swim, Rainbow and I still have a chance to win the whole tournament if we do well on the trail run. Plus, Saskia and her team finished fourth in the Dragon Dash—so they're definitely within catch-up distance. I've been practicing by hiking The Twins a couple of times a week, a trail a few minutes away from our flat that goes all the way to Stanley. It's called The Twins because it has two equally high hills—it's 500 steps up the first hill and another 500 up the second, with nowhere to go if you change your mind once you're in the valley between them.

I see Rainbow heading to the library and I sprint to catch

up to her. "You're just the person I was looking for. Do you want to hike Twins after school today? Or maybe run to Repulse Bay along the reservoir?"

"Oh, sorry, I can't. I'm meeting my eco-art group. We're starting to make the backdrop for the Flower Fair photo booth. We're using materials we found at the beach cleanup. It's going to be really cool—both a way to show how we can reuse and upcycle the waste, but also to highlight all the waste that washes up every tide."

"That sounds really cool, but can't they start the backdrop without you? And you can join next week after the race? We need to train."

"I don't need to train, Holly-Mei. I've done the Eight Immortals with my mom a couple of times already."

"Yes, but this time it's a race." I feel like I need to remind her that this isn't some jolly stroll in the park.

"Yes, but we're just doing it *for fun*, right? Those were the exact words you used, remember?" She raises her eyebrows at me.

I'm tired of people who don't try hard but still win, like Millie and her baking contest. And maybe even more so, people who expect to compete without trying. I bet that we could have done better in the Dragon Dash if we had practiced more. And now I'm behind Saskia. I need to do well in this race to beat her. It's my turn to win for once.

I say, "Look, the backdrop is just a bunch of garbage that they're putting together and calling art. How hard is that? Why do you need to be there? This race is more important."

"You know what's garbage, Holly-Mei? Your attitude. You say you're in it for fun, but you're not. You're too intense. Too competitive. Why do you care so much about winning?"

My jaw clenches as my mind flashes back to that conversation with Ah-ma when she said that I need to do that "zi zhi zhi ming" thing, recognize my strengths and weaknesses. That some people have talents I can't match, no matter how hard I practice, namely Millie and Saskia.

"I'm tired of people always doing better than me." I practically spit the words out.

"What do you mean by *doing better*?" Rainbow challenges.

"People who win trophies and competitions." I don't know how this isn't more obvious to her.

"I do sports because it's fun. I do eco-art club because it's fun. But this race has become no fun at all." She puts her hands on her hips.

"What are you saying?" I ask as my eyes narrow.

"I'm saying I'm quitting the race." Her tone is low and

even. I hear everything, but at the same time I don't understand.

"What? You're pulling out?" A dull ache forms in my stomach and spreads quickly all over my body.

"Pulling out? No, Holly-Mei, you've pushed me out. You can do this race solo. It's just an average of our times, so you don't need me. Besides, I have an eco-art exhibition I'd rather attend."

I feel the tickle in my nose that happens right before I start to cry. I want to get out of here before the hot tears fall. "You're right. I don't need you. Have fun with your eco-*garbage* group." I turn and march to the nearest bathroom, where I stay until my eyes are empty of falling tears.

I hike home from school over The Twins, and according to my sports watch, I get my best time ever, but it doesn't feel like an accomplishment. I text Rosie—I really need to talk to her, to hear her say something soothing in that gentle voice of hers—but I can tell that she hasn't picked up my messages. When I reach Lofty Heights, I go straight to her tower instead of mine. The familiar sound of the Big Ben doorbell chimes and Rhys opens the door.

"Hey!" he says. "Rosie's not here. Come in. I'm trying out that new FIFA video game. Want to have a go?"

"No thanks, I've got some math review to do. Where's Rosie?"

"She's out somewhere with Henry."

My heart sinks. She's spending so much of her time with Henry and now she's missing right when I really need her. How could she abandon me like this? First Rainbow, now Rosie?

"Are you okay? Your eyes and face are all red."

I wave it off. "Yes, I just hiked here, so I'm really tired." I give him a smile to show that I appreciate his concern. He's the only person who has asked me about my feelings today. "Just tell her I stopped by. I'll message her too."

We wave goodbye and I head down in the lift and back home in the next tower.

I compose a text to her, about needing to chat, asking her to come by later. But I read it over and over before deciding to delete it. Instead, I just type *Popped by. You were out.* What if she agrees with Rainbow? Did I really push her away? I thought my plan was so perfect, but it's ending up costing me a good friend. My head starts to throb with all the thoughts zooming through it.

I enter our flat and for the first time, it feels cold and damp. It's even colder because I'm still wearing my exercise clothes, which are a bit wet with sweat. Mom and Dad had already explained that there isn't normally heat-

ing in Hong Kong apartments in winter, just air condition-
ing, since winter can sometimes last only a few weeks
and it rarely gets colder than ten degrees Celsius or fifty
degrees Fahrenheit. But the chill in the flat is unsettling,
unwelcoming.

A text from Dad flashes on my screen. *I just popped
into town to get us a few space heaters for the bedrooms.
[Snowman emoji]. Mom's working late but I'll be back soon.
[Smiley face emoji].*

I don't have the energy to text anything so I just send
him a heart emoji. In my room, I pull off my damp clothes
and jump into the shower. The rush of hot water against
my throbbing head is soothing. The eucalyptus scent of
the shampoo fills my senses and I feel my mind clear. I
know I should limit my shower time to save water, but I
don't want to leave my steamy cocoon. I turn my face to
the rushing water and let the rain shower massage my
face, and I imagine I'm at the Peninsula spa, like Millie
was at Lizzie Lo's birthday party, tranquil, without a care
in the world.

My bathroom door bangs open. "Hols, I need your help."
Millie is standing on the marble tiles in an apron, covered
with flour. I turn off the shower and grab a towel. "Oh my
God, are you okay? Did you hurt yourself?"

"No, I'm fine."

"Did you burn the kitchen down?"

"Of course not."

"Then, what's the problem? Why do you need help?"

"I'm trying to get the perfect angle for a selfie with my new cream-filled creation, but my arm is too short. I need you to be my selfie stick."

More like *selfish* stick, I think. But I'm too tired and drained to argue with her. Helping her will keep my mind occupied and off my own troubles. I throw on leggings, a hoodie, and some cozy socks covered in Moomins.

I push the kitchen door open and cannot believe what I'm seeing. Flour suspended in the air, like a fog. Sugar, white, brown, in crystals and chunks, splayed over the granite kitchen counters. Mixing bowls of every size rimmed with goo and filled with whisks, spatulas, and spoons.

"What on earth are you doing?" I ask, astonished.

"Come look." She points at the concoction on the kitchen island. It looks like a seafoam green wedding cake layered with pastel pink garlands. "Does it look good? I've been working on this for hours."

"It's crooked."

"I know. Isn't it great? I call it the Leaning Tower of Millie."

"It looks like something the Little Mermaid would serve at her wedding."

"Really?" Millie seems to take this as a compliment.

"Do Dad and Joy know what you're up to?" I ask.

"Dad's still shopping, and Joy's out with her cousin. Come, help me take a photo before it falls over." She takes her dirty apron off, fluffs her hair, and applies a coat of lip gloss.

I stand on a chair and take a few photos of Millie and her creation from a variety of angles. She grabs her phone back and chooses a photo, applies a filter, and posts it. "Voila. Now the likes better come rolling in."

"Millie, you've been baking something new every day since you won that competition."

"I know. I have to keep posting new stuff."

"No, you don't. You used to love to bake, just for the baking bit. Now you're obsessed with the number of likes you get. It's not a competition."

"You don't know what you're talking about. And who's the one going around always talking about winning?" She points her finger at me, wagging it in time with her words. "You, Holly-Mei, that's who." She puts both her hands on her hips, making her look a little like Mom does when she's mad.

"That's different, Millie. I'm in a *real* competition."

Her eyes open wide with disbelief, as if I said something totally outlandish.

"Why do you want to win so badly, Holly-Mei? Is it because you want people to like you?"

"Shut up, Millie."

"Or are you just jealous of me? That I won something and you haven't. Is that why you're so desperate to win?"

"You said you didn't care about winning that stupid baking contest. You completely forgot about it and you didn't even have butter! But oh-so-talented Millie makes up a recipe and without even trying, you win! Now you're Little Miss Baking Champion, everyone wants to be your friend, and you're all over the school paper, Instagram, and now the Flower Fair!"

I grab a tangerine from the fruit bowl and throw it at her. My frustrations about everything—Millie's talent, Saskia's skill, and my loss of friendship with Rainbow—propel the tangerine forward with more momentum than I expected. Millie tries to catch it but it rebounds out of her hands and flies toward the cake.

SPLAT!

It hits the top tier and the leaning cake starts to lean even more. It stops moving and seems to stabilize and we take a deep breath. Then it suddenly starts to keel over and I rush to one side and try to hold it steady.

"Save it, Hols!" Millie cries.

"I'm trying," I say, my hands planted on the side of the cake.

But the cake keeps leaning and leaning further until the top tier breaks off—Millie catches it. We look back and forth at each other, me practically wrist-deep into the cake, her with a full tier cupped in her hands. I feel terrible that I've ruined her creation. I hear Millie starting to cry and I feel even worse.

"Millie?" I ask tentatively.

But after a few seconds, I realize she's not crying. She's laughing. I can tell by her snort.

"Oh my God, Hols, now that would have made an amazing video. It would have gone viral for sure."

"I'm sorry about the cake." I really mean it.

"It's okay. I got the photo. That's the most important bit, isn't it?"

She takes a bite of the cake in her hands. "Hmmm, tasty." She holds her arms out to me. "Here, try it."

"You're not going to squish it in my face, are you?" I pull my head away.

"I hadn't thought of it, but now that you mention it—" She snorts again.

I take a small bite and then another bigger one. It's amazingly delicious. The sponge is so moist and has a tiny kick to it. "Did you put fresh ginger in here?"

She nods.

"Millie, you know you're really talented, right?"

"I know." She puts the top tier down on a plate and helps me straighten the base. "But thanks for saying it. Sometimes I forget why I do it, you know, when I'm so busy posting and stuff."

"And you're right. I think I am a bit envious of you." It's a relief to say out loud.

"Hols, I may be good in the kitchen. And with makeup. But you're good at so many other things, like math and sports. It's okay that we're good at different things." She licks the icing off her finger.

I wash my hands and take a photo of her, surrounded by the mess, icing in her hands and her hair. "Post this. No filter. The real you."

"I don't know. What if people don't like it?"

"If they don't like the real you, then you shouldn't care what they think."

She nods and does as I say. Then she comes over and gives me a big hug.

"You're going to help me clean up before everyone gets home, right?"

"For sure," I say as I start clearing the counter.

# 16

The lunch bell rings and I spot Rosie and Henry down the hall. She's playing with her long blond hair, which she has been wearing down lately instead of in her usual ballet bun. He is leaning against her locker and they are both laughing. It seems like every time I look for her, she's with him. She says that they're just friends, but they definitely have a crush on each other. They even sat on the bus together this morning. Henry sat in *my* seat and Rosie didn't ask him to move—it was like she didn't even see me. I had to sit with her brother and he talked my ear off about his new best player on FIFA Ultimate Team.

It's bad enough that I never see Rosie anymore, and she's not even dating Henry yet! If that happens, I'm afraid that I'm going to fade to invisibility.

I pull out my lunch bag from the bottom of my knapsack. I'm glad I brought a packed lunch—a Tupperware full of Millie's collapsed cake, a cheese sandwich and an apple, plus a book. I wait until the others have all walked in the direction of the cafeteria and I head instead to the roof terrace. I don't want to deal with the crowd at lunch. And I definitely don't want to face Rainbow. I pull the hood of my Tai Tam Prep hoodie over my head to keep my ears warm against the wind and start my lunch by eating the cake. Even though the clouds are gray, the cake gives me a comforting warmth, like Millie's wrapping me in a hug.

Straight after the dismissal bell, Rosie approaches me in the hallway.

"Let's grab some bubble tea at the beach." She catches me a bit off-guard—I wasn't expecting a nice invitation.

"I need to train. The race is on Saturday."

"Are you sure? You've been working so hard. Maybe one day off would be good for you? Please?"

I am exhausted, mentally and physically. Maybe an afternoon of me and Rosie, like old times, will help. "That sounds like a good idea. Let's do it." My shoulders straighten and I feel a little taller already. I hadn't realized I was hunched over all day.

Then Rosie says, "Henry has a sailing class."

I want to ask, *So, you're only hanging out with me because*

*Henry's busy?* But instead, I say, "Too bad he can't join us." She doesn't pick up on my teeny touch of sarcasm. I really shouldn't use that tone—Dad says that sarcasm is the lowest form of humor. But it kind of felt good to try and give a little jab, so she could experience how I was feeling, even though it flew over her head.

We get off the bus and head to the beachfront plaza at Repulse Bay. The wind has picked up and we both shove our hands inside the pockets of our hoodies to keep them warm. The beach is empty, the water is choppy, and the plaza is practically deserted. We are the only customers sitting inside the bubble tea café. Rosie orders a regular milk tea with pearl, half sugar. I get the taro milk with pearl, no ice. Taro is my new discovery—it's like a purple sweet potato and it tastes a bit like coconut.

"Share an egg waffle?" I ask. Eating cake at lunch makes me crave more cake.

"Yum, yes please!"

The man at the counter fills the steel mold with batter and shuts it. As we wait, I drink my lavender-colored concoction through a wide paper straw and chew on the gelatinous balls. Not too soft, but not hard. Just right. We stare at the fragrant steam coming out the sides of the waffle iron. The man cuts the excess batter off the edges before he opens the lid and plops what I could only describe as a golden pancake full of golf-ball-sized puffs on a plate. We each tear out a ball and pop it in our mouths. It's crunchy on the outside and chewy but airy on the inside.

"So good," I say with my mouth half full.

I wolf down my half of the egg waffle, but Rosie is picking at hers. I can tell something's on her mind.

"Everything okay?" I ask.

"Rhys told me you stopped by yesterday. I got your text, but I was home so late."

"Out with Henry?" This time I raise my eyebrows, to see if she reacts and can read what I'm thinking: *You're always with Henry. You never have time left for me. I really needed to talk to you yesterday.*

"Yes, we were hanging out at Stanley Plaza."

Clearly, she does not have the gift of reading minds.

"I saw Rainbow at lunch today." She pauses and looks down like she's concentrating hard on the contents of her plate. "She told me that she pulled out of the tournament." She looks up and asks, "Are you okay?"

"What did she say?" My back stiffens as I wait for whatever insults might be relayed.

"That you were too intense." Rosie bites her lip.

"Do you think she's right?" I can tell my tone is too assertive. Her eyes go wide like that emoji. I soften it by saying, "It's okay. Just tell me what you really think."

Rosie doesn't like to say anything that might make people upset, but I can read it on her face, in her silence. If we had talked yesterday when I went over, I would have been full-steaming mad at Rainbow. But after the leaning cake incident and thinking back to what Millie asked, about why I wanted to win so badly, maybe there was a bit of truth in what both she and Rainbow said. Maybe I'm mistaken thinking that winning will make my friends like me more. People certainly seem to like me better when I don't care about winning.

And what about me being envious of Millie's talent? It was a huge relief to admit it out loud yesterday—how annoying it is for me that some things come to her easily even when she doesn't try. And what about when I yelled at her about baking for likes? I love sports because I love being active and being on a team. I like to win, but it doesn't drive me. Until now, that is. When everyone else started winning, I felt like I was being left behind. But now it's driving my friend Rainbow away.

"I said something mean about her art." I cringe at the memory of me calling her beloved club the *eco-garbage group*. "I wouldn't be surprised if she doesn't talk to me ever again."

"Reach out to her. I'm sure you can work things out." Her tone is reassuring.

"And is that why you're not hanging out with me? Because I'm too intense?"

"What do you mean? I had a great time at the Dragon Dash on Saturday." She sounds surprised and genuine.

"But you're always with Henry."

"Not always," she says in a slightly defensive tone.

"Ever since we came back from Christmas break, you're always at your locker with him, hanging out with him, making popcorn with him. And you're only hanging out with me now because he's not free this afternoon." My voice goes quiet. "I feel like I'm slowly losing my best friend."

"Holly-Mei, you're definitely not losing me. I just like being around him." She pauses. "Do I really make you feel that way?" Her voice is almost a whisper and her eyes turn glassy. "I'm sorry for being a bad friend."

I reach over and hold her hand. "And I'm sorry for being so, you know, Holly-Mei-ish."

She laughs and squeezes my hand. We sit there like that as we sip the last drops of our bubble tea, the straws making a sucking sound.

"Let's both agree to try and do better with everyone," I say and she nods in agreement. "And you think Rainbow will take me back as a friend?"

"I think so. I would." She smiles warmly. "I almost forgot. I want to show you something." She pulls her phone out of her bag, turns it horizontally, and presses *play*. "It's the video Snowy made of the Dragon Dash. She just finished editing it."

The Bruno Mars song "Count on Me" starts playing. I see clips of our team in matching thunderbolt tops and capes smiling, laughing, and cheering each other on.

"You did this. You brought our team together," she says.

The lyrics are so simple—about friends counting on each other—but they make so much sense. We didn't just have fun. We were a team. A team of friends. Supporting each other through the ups and downs, like we're supposed to do. And we had so much fun at the barbecue afterward, even though we didn't win.

Rainbow is right. It is about having fun. I need to fix this. Now.

★ ★ ★

The next morning, the sun is shining brightly and the sky is no longer gray. This is a sign it's going to be a good day. I crunch on my apple slices and munch on my peanut-butter-and-jam toast. Breakfast of champions.

"Try these." Millie passes me a small container of cookies. "If you like them, I can make you a fresh batch before your race on Saturday. They have banana, oats, and chocolate, so they'll give you lots of energy."

"When did you bake these?"

"Yesterday, after school."

"I didn't see a new post from you."

"I didn't take a photo. I just baked. Like old times. Oh, and I added a touch of cardamom too."

I sniff the cookies. "They smell like Christmas." I take another sniff. "Hmm, so good."

"I know, right?"

"Thanks, Millie. This is really thoughtful of you."

When we arrive at school, I see Rainbow walking toward the library on her own. Now is my chance to talk with her before classes start. I run to catch up, but I stay two steps behind, still ruminating over what exactly to say. She turns sharply on her heels and faces me.

"Are you following me?" she asks. I can't tell if she's mad or not, but by her furrowed brow, she looks more confused than annoyed. "I saw your reflection in the glass over there," she says pointing down the hall.

"I was hoping we could talk before the bell."

"About the tournament?"

"Yes, the tournament, my intensity, and—" I pause to gather up the courage "—and my rudeness. About your art. I'm sorry. It was a crummy thing for me to say. A crummy friend for me to be."

Rainbow's face relaxes. "I'm sorry too. I shouldn't have pulled out. I'll run the race with you this weekend."

This takes me by surprise and I'm tempted. But I know her heart's not really in it. "It's okay. You go to your eco-art exhibition. I can do the race on my own."

"Are you sure?"

"Totally. Our times would be averaged out anyway. But only as long as you promise to send me positive vibes on the day."

"Pinky promise." We both start giggling as we lock our pinky fingers together.

After school, I head out to the field hockey pitch to hit a few balls. It's been weeks since I've held a stick and it feels so comfortable in my hand—like it's an old friend. Dev is on the other side of the pitch about to help coach some of the younger students for the after-school club.

He waves and comes over. "Hey, I was looking for you earlier."

"You were?"

"I wanted to give you something." He reaches into his bag and pulls out a gel pack. "For your race. It's an energy gel."

"You think I'll need it?"

"Not if you were just on a regular hike of the Eight Immortals Trail, but this is a race and you'll be pushing yourself more than you're used to. So, make sure you keep it until you're a few hours in, just in case you need an energy boost. Trust me."

"Chocolate mint flavor! My favorite."

"I know." He winks at me, throws his bag over his shoulder, and runs back toward the little kids.

# 17

Today is *the* day. The culmination of this roller coaster of a month. The race along the Eight Immortals Trail up in Pat Sin Leng. Twelve kilometers and three and a half hours of effort.

Yesterday, my friends sat me down to give me a pep session. Rainbow described the trail in detail. "The first couple of kilometers are flat. Then it's hard-core stairs for about an hour. Then the incline becomes less steep. After two and a half hours, you'll reach the peaks of the Eight Immortals Trail. That's the fun up-and-down part, then it's all downhill and flat to the finish line."

Theo and Dev jostled to share advice, while Gemma gave them both some side-eye.

"You can run the flat parts, no problem. Be careful running on the downhill, especially if you're tired," Theo said.

"Or if it's wet," Dev chimed in. "And don't forget the gel pack. It will help you over the finish line."

"And you'll need lots of water," Theo said.

Dev interjects again with, "At least two liters."

I laughed at their need to talk over each other.

"Any other words of wisdom from you two?" Gemma asked, eyebrows raised. They both shook their heads. "Good, because I think she's got this," she said with a confident nod in my direction.

"I've volunteered to be one of the photographers at the finish line." Snowy pretended to take my photo with her imaginary camera.

"And we'll be at the finish line to celebrate," said Rosie, as she clapped her hands.

"I feel like a winner already, guys. Thank you."

Now, I'm sitting at the dining table as Dad brings me my breakfast: a bowl of porridge with chopped-up walnuts and maple syrup drizzled on top and a glass of freshly squeezed orange juice.

"I researched the best meal to give you energy throughout the day," he says, taking a seat beside me. "This is what's recommended for marathoners."

Mom brings out a pot of Earl Grey tea and pours a cup for herself and Dad before sitting down across from me.

"I'm very proud of you for doing this race. Being so focused on training. It's a lot at your age." She pats my hand.

I don't tell her I've been *too* dedicated and focused, particularly on winning. I know better now, but I wonder how she feels about the possibility of me *not* winning. Mom seems to be good at whatever she does—tennis, piano, work—like Millie and her baking.

"Mom, what if I don't win?" I ask delicately, a little afraid of the answer.

"That's absolutely okay." She looks at me, her eyes wide like she's surprised at my question.

"Really?"

"Yes, of course. I'm proud of your dedication. Do your best and I'll be proud of you no matter the result."

"Even if she comes in last?" Millie walks toward the table, bowl in hand, and spoons some porridge in her mouth before sitting down.

"Even if she comes in last. All I ask," she looks to Dad and then corrects herself, "all *we* ask, is that you try your best in everything you do. And this includes schoolwork, girls. We want real effort. But if you fall down—and you *will* fall down and make mistakes—your father and I are here to help you pick up the pieces and stand up again."

I look at Dad and he laughs and points at Mom. "Exactly what she said. First place, 100th place, you're always a winner to me, poppet." He gets up and kisses me on the head. "Just do your best and stay safe."

"Oh, before I forget, we know how much you love hiking, so we thought you could use some new equipment for today." Mom gets up and returns a few seconds later with a small sleek, streamlined bag.

"Oh! A CamelBak." I've always wanted a bag like this, with a built-in water pack. "Now I don't need to lug four water bottles with me."

"It was actually Millie's idea," Dad says.

I look at her and she just shrugs. "I thought you should look the part. It wears like a vest." She tries it on and twirls around. "And it has a pocket for your phone and one for these." She hands me a ziplock bag of her freshly baked oatmeal banana chocolate chip cookies.

I get up and give Millie a big hug. Her kindness surprises me. We don't say anything, but the warmth of our embrace says enough.

A half an hour later, we are all piled into the van with Ah-Lok for the long drive to the New Territories, one of the three areas that make up the city of Hong Kong—the other two being Kowloon and Hong Kong Island, where we live. Compared to Repulse Bay, which is at the southern end of Hong Kong, the New Territories is the northern end, and shares a border with Mainland China. I checked the map yesterday and Dad gave us a rundown of the area's history, like how it's called *New*, but it's really been part of Hong Kong since 1899.

I do a check of everything in my new bag—Millie's cookies, Dev's gel pack, tissues, hat, sunglasses, lip balm, Band-Aids, hand sanitizer, and my phone. And then I redo it because I'm so nervous and have lost track of what I've just checked.

"Do you have sunscreen, honey?" Mom asks.

I groan and tell her I've already put some on. "What? Just checking," she says.

"What about your earphones?" Dad asks.

"No, I just want to listen to my surroundings," I say. I find the sound of leaves rustling and footsteps crunching soothing.

Millie is looking out the window, pointing at the scenery, and asking questions. We all stare at her in bemused surprise. Normally her eyes are glued to her phone.

"My, you're curious today. Phone out of battery already?" Dad jokes, turning his head from the front passenger seat.

"I didn't bring my phone. I thought I'd take a bit of a break."

Mom and Dad face each other and smile widely.

"That is a wonderful idea." Mom gently strokes Millie's head.

After just over an hour, we get off the highway and meander through small villages, past little organic farms and strawberry patches until we reach Hok Tau. The racers are gathered at the cul-de-sac where the road ends and the trail begins. We get out of the van and Mom helps me pin on my race bib with the embedded time chip. I feel a little chilly in shorts and a sports T-shirt, so I start jumping and running on the spot to warm up.

"Remember to stretch so you don't injure yourself," Dad says. Good idea—I start touching my toes and stretching my calves. "You said there were safety checkpoints, right?"

"Yes, there are teachers posted along the trail."

"I'll have a clean T-shirt and hoodie for you at the finish line," Mom says.

"Just try your best, but if you get tired, it's okay to stop and rest. Safety first. Walk if you need to," Dad says. I look at Mom and she says with a smile, "What your father said." They give me a big hug and my nervousness dissipates. I'm determined to do this race just for fun.

But, as I'm hugging my parents, I see Saskia to the side, staring at us, almost with a longing expression. I untangle myself from my parents and give her a nod. Something about seeing her kitted out in her pink-and-royal-blue trail running shoes and mirrored sports sunglasses makes the fire of competitiveness in my stomach roar back to life, as if she were the puff of oxygen on some dying embers. I don't know why I care about beating her in this race so much.

I feel a tug on my elbow and get pulled back into the pre-race chatter around me.

"Hey, what's up?" Millie asks. I realize that I've just been standing still and not stretching.

"She's so good at hockey in a way I know I'll never be, no matter how hard I try," I say, looking in Saskia's direction. "So I feel like I need to beat her to prove I'm not some big failure."

"Don't worry about her or anyone else. Just do it for you, Holly-Mei Jones," Millie whispers. Sometimes she can be so wise for someone who's only eleven.

I nod in agreement. "That sounds like a perfect plan."

Mom, Dad, and Millie tell me they'll be waiting for me at the finish line, and we do another group hug before they head back to the van.

I make a port-a-loo pit stop beside the race start area. On the way there, I see Saskia with her parents. I hear them say things like: *start strong and leave them in the dust; if you're tired just push through it;* and *Olympic-sized effort.* I want to go grab her hand and pull her away from the awful cloud of energy that is hanging over her. I'm so thankful that my parents don't put pressure on me like that.

It's the two-minute countdown to the race. I take a sip

of water through the tube in my CamelBak and check my phone one last time and I see a bunch of messages from my friends, all wishing me luck. With friends like that, I feel like luck is already on my side.

# 18

The starting horn goes and the pack of racers take off running. I see Saskia shoot out in front, but I keep to a modest running pace—I don't want to push myself this early, especially after what Rainbow told me about what's lying ahead. And she was right. The stairs after the first couple of kilometers are hard-core. The incline is as steep as on The Twins, but the steps seem to go on forever. Even though Millie's cookies and Dad's porridge are giving me lots of energy and the excitement of the race keeps me moving quickly, my legs are burning and my breath heaving. When I think I've reached the end of the stairs, there always seems to be yet another twist, like the mountain is saying, *gotcha!* So, I've decided to just look at my feet and concentrate on putting one foot in front of the other. I'm being passed on the side by some people, but that's okay. I'm going at my own pace and this is as fast as I can go.

After more than an hour, I reach the first safety checkpoint and finally make it to the top of the steps. In front of me is a breathtaking scene—a chalky white trail that undulates along the ridge of the range, like a pearl necklace laid across emerald satin. It makes the pain of the last hour worth it. My new bag has pockets in the front, so I don't need to take it off to reach for my phone, and I snap a few photos without losing any time.

I see Tsz Shan Monastery in the distance with its giant white statue of Guanyin, the Goddess of Mercy, standing like a beacon of light. Dad told me it's double the size of the Big Buddha statue on Lantau and one of the tallest statues in the world. On the other side, I can see the Mainland Chinese city of Shenzhen where Millie and I went shopping with Rosie and her mom in the autumn.

The sun is shining and there are no clouds, but it's not too hot and my hat keeps my eyes shaded. I walk the gentler incline of the ridge briskly and run the downhills. I even pass some people who had sprinted ahead of me earlier, but who are now running out of energy. I pat the gel pack in the pocket of my bag. This is my secret weapon for later.

I come across a wooden signpost with the name and

outline of the trail carved into it, indicating the start of the Eight Immortals section of the trail, Pat Sin Leng 八仙嶺. There are eight peaks, each named after one of the group of eight saintlike spirits from Chinese mythology—they are said to be able to bestow blessings and vanquish evil. Compared to the first hill I had to climb to get to the ridge, these peaks and troughs are gentle and the views even more spectacular—the sea, dotted with hilly green islands, lies ahead. The scenery looks so quiet and peaceful, it's hard to believe that millions of people live less than an hour away.

I come up to the second-last peak and see one of the racers sitting on a bench. My heart skips a beat when I see the familiar pink-and-royal-blue trail running shoes, now covered in white dust. Saskia Okoh is taking a break! And I'm going to pass her! Even though there's no way I'm going to win this race, it feels great to achieve this small victory. There's now a little spring in my step.

But there's something about Saskia's posture that tells me she's not okay—she's leaning forward, her head gripped between her hands, and her mirrored sports sunglasses lying in the dust at her feet. I stop and bend my knees so I'm eye level with her.

"Saskia? Are you okay?"

"I can't do this." She looks up and her face is red and blotchy.

"Of course you can. You're the best athlete in our grade." It's something I've never admitted out loud, but I can't deny it anymore. I pull her hand gently to try and get her up.

"I'm so tired. My legs. My body. My head." She leans back on the bench like she's flopping on the sofa, and I sit down beside her, scanning the area for a teacher or adult, but I can't see anyone.

"Hey, what would your parents say? *Push through it*." I repeat what I heard them say at the start line, hoping it would energize her. But apparently, it's the worst thing I could have said.

"My parents? They're the ones making me so tired." Thick tears flow down her face. "I'm not going to win this race and I don't want to face them at the finish line."

I pass her a tissue, crumpled but clean, from my bag pocket and she blows her nose.

"My parents only care about me winning and their bragging rights. Their 'Olympic material daughter.'" She scoffs and looks up at the sky as if talking to the air. "They don't care about what I want."

A sharper, clearer image of Saskia appears, like I can finally see her as who she is—just a regular twelve-year-old girl with her own dreams, rather than the competitive archnemesis that I've imagined her to be. The patter of footsteps as people run past us fills my ears, but I ignore it. I reach into my pocket and pull out my chocolate mint energy gel pack. Dev said I would need it, but it sounds like Saskia needs it more than I do.

"Here. This should give you a boost. And it's bound to be yummy too."

"Are you sure?"

"Yes, totally. I ate a bunch of oatmeal cookies my sister made. I'm good. Plus, it's going to be downhill after the next peak."

"Thank you." She tries to open it but her hands are shaking too much.

"Here, let me help." I rip it open and pass it to her. She smiles and eats the whole thing in one gulp. She motions for me to leave and says with her mouth still gooey, "Go, run. You can catch those people."

"You sure?"

"Yes, go."

I give her a little pat on the shoulder like Ah-ma used to do to cheer me up. "I think you need to tell your parents how you really feel. They might surprise you."

"Maybe." She gives a little shrug and a smile. "And, Holly-Mei? Thank you. You're a very thoughtful friend."

I wave bye to her and start running down the steps toward the last peak. Her words echo in my head, *a very thoughtful friend*. No one has commended me for being thoughtful before. I didn't even have to try that hard—the thought of giving her the gel pack just came to me. Maybe because I wasn't focused on winning.

I skip-run up the last peak—Hsien Ku Fung, named after Ho Hsien-ku, the beautiful fairylike deity among the Eight Immortals. I can picture the painting Ah-ma made of her that was hanging in our house in Toronto, with her cascading hair and flowing robes, holding a giant lotus flower. I take one last photo of the gorgeous scenery that I'll send to Ah-ma when I reach the finish line.

It's all downhill and flat from here. I've passed at least a dozen people on my way up and I even pass a few more as I skip my way down the steps, careful not to slip or twist my ankle. When I reach the bottom, a sign tells me I have just over three kilometers left in the race. The terrain here is so different from the exposed ridge and peak. The trail is now flat and inside the canopy of the forest. I didn't think the sun was strong, but it's a relief to be sheltered from it, although it takes a while for my eyes to adjust.

As I run gingerly over the tree roots and rocks that are littering the trail, I think about how not being focused on winning, but instead on just doing my best at my own pace, has made this a better race than I could have imagined. And more importantly, I did something thoughtful, for someone I hope I can get to know better. Maybe we'll become good friends.

I can hear a loudspeaker and some cheering. The finish line! I'm almost there. I can see the end of the trail a couple of hundred meters ahead through a gap in the trees. The sun also manages to break through the canopy and I turn my face to peek at the sky. The leaves are rustling, the birds are singing, and I'm flying. Flying through the air, that is.

And then BAM. I land on the ground with a hard thud.

During that one second of inattention, I must have tripped on an exposed tree root and am now on my hands and knees on the forest floor. I crawl to the side of the trail and lean against a tree as I try and catch my breath. Runners, who either can't see me or are assuming I'm just having a rest, pass me by. My palms sting and little pinprick-size spots of blood start to appear, which I wipe away on my legs. I can see the shiny surface of raw skin on my knees, and my left ankle is throbbing.

I grab onto the tree and slowly start to stand up, never letting go, putting all my weight on my right foot. After all I've accomplished, not only today but during the whole tournament—bringing my friends together and even making a new one—I feel like I have to finish. I *need* to finish. But my left ankle buckles under the slightest bit of weight. I blink away tears.

I can only watch as the other racers leave me in their dust.

# 19

I lean back against the tree standing on one leg, close my eyes and take deep breaths. The whooshing of runners going by is magnified in my head so that it sounds like the winds of a typhoon. I hear someone yell, "You okay?" as they run by and I put my thumb up to indicate I'm fine. I don't want someone to ruin their race by stopping to help me this close to the finish line.

I'm determined to continue. I try and gingerly put weight on my left foot again and searing pain shoots up my leg. But I find if I hold on to a tree and hop on my right leg, I can move little by little. It may take me ten minutes to hop to the finish line, but I'm going to do it.

"Hey, you're hurt." It's Saskia, her eyebrows creased with concern.

"Don't worry, nothing's broken." I rotate my left ankle to show her. "I think I just twisted it. But why are you stopped? Go!" I point to the finish line up ahead.

"I'm not leaving you to hobble on your own." She places my arm around her shoulders so that I can use her as a crutch.

"But the race—" I don't want her to get into any trouble with her parents.

"My mind is made up." She puts her arm around my torso.

This is what it feels like to be on the receiving end of a thoughtful friend. I guess I never paid much attention before to the acts of kindness that people did for me.

We manage a good pace with me bouncing on one leg and her propping me up and propelling me forward. After a couple of minutes, I'm able to put a bit of weight on my foot, and I manage to turn my hops into more of a hobble. Runners who pass us give us a little clap or cheer as they go by. We reach the end of the dirt path and take the steps down to the Spring Breeze Pavilion. The crowd comes into view and the cheering seems to intensify. I swear I can hear my and Saskia's name being called out.

"Just a few more steps," she says.

We cross the finish line, passing under an arch of twisted red-and-white balloons, the colors of the Hong Kong flag.

"We did it!" I say, hugging Saskia.

"We made a great team," she says, hugging me back.

Mom, Dad, and Millie come running up with a multitude of questions.

"Are you hurt?"

"What happened?"

"Do you need a doctor?"

"I'm fine, really. Thanks to Saskia," I say as Dad steadies me. My parents thank her profusely.

"I'll go find you some ice," Saskia says.

Dad helps me away from the crowd and eases me onto the curb to sit while Mom takes my left shoe off and has a look at my ankle.

"Nothing that rest and a bit of Tiger Balm won't fix," Mom announces.

Rosie, Henry, Dev, Theo, Rhys, and Snowy with a camera around her neck all gather and congratulate me for finishing the race and the tournament.

"Rainbow! You made it," I say as she pushes her way through the crowd.

"The eco-art exhibit was good but I wanted to be here with you to celebrate the end of the tournament."

"How does it feel to be done?" Rosie asks me.

"Amazing. Even though I probably came in last today." It's strange how just a few days ago, this would've really upset me. But I feel nothing but proud now. Helping Saskia and being helped in return has given me a better feeling than winning ever could.

"Actually, you and Saskia tied for eighteenth place. That's pretty good considering you hobbled over the finish line." Dev flashes me the race results page on his phone.

"And you came in eighth in the whole tournament! Saskia came in third."

"That's fantastic, on all counts," I say.

I look around for Saskia. I spot her close by, just outside the first aid tent, holding a dripping bag of ice in one hand and gesturing in frustration with the other. She's talking to her parents and they don't look happy. I hear her being challenged: *Why would you slow down to help a competitor? Don't you know it cost you valuable time?* But I hear her stand up for herself and tell them how I helped her. How she wouldn't even have finished if it weren't for me. How they need to stop pressuring her or she's going to stop doing hockey altogether. My eyes go wide upon hearing this. But there's too much noise and I don't catch what happens next.

Saskia comes back with the ice and places it on my ankle.

"That was really brave," I whisper.

"I had to say it." She doesn't look happy and I don't ask anything more about it, even though I'm dying to know how her parents reacted. I keep my questions in my head, filtering my thoughts to keep them from flying out of my mouth.

Coach Kelly gets on the loudspeaker and hands out the medals for the day, congratulating everyone for participating and making the trail race event and the whole tournament a success. Everyone erupts in cheers.

"And I have another award to hand out. It's one that wasn't on the agenda but under the circumstances, we, the organizing committee, felt we needed to add it. The winners of this award embody what we value in sport, but sometimes lose sight of when we're overly concerned with winning, breaking records, and accumulating medals. What I'm talking about is good sportsmanship. Being a good citizen and helping each other collectively when it means maybe losing out individually. It's my honor to present the Good Sportsmanship Award for the Grade 7 Inter-School Tri Tournament to Holly-Mei Jones and Saskia Okoh!"

Our mouths drop open and we squeal with delight, hugging each other again. Saskia helps me up and I hobble over with her to the podium. Coach Kelly puts us on the first place step, where we stand hand in hand. He en-

courages another round of cheering from the crowd—
Mom and Dad are clapping and Millie is jumping up and
down. And I see Saskia's parents, both smiling proudly
and giving their daughter a thumbs-up.

# 20

Over my black leggings, I put on the violet-hued qipao dress that Mom picked up for me in the Lanes in Central—a couple of pedestrian alleys between blocks of high-rises lined with little green-painted stalls selling clothes and shoes. This time of year, many of the stalls have satinlike Chinese-style jackets and dresses in a rainbow of colors and patterns, all with distinctive knotted buttons. This is the only time that we're allowed to come to school without our Tai Tam Prep uniforms on. For the whole week leading up to the Lunar New Year, we can wear Chinese-style or other Asian traditional clothes.

Yesterday, I wore Mom's golden silk jacket with green knotted buttons and some jeans, but today is the day of the Lunar New Year Flower Fair—we were so happy the school listened to our suggestion to change the name of the event—and I decide to wear the new dress, which makes Mom pinch my cheeks and comment how I should wear dresses more often.

In the kitchen, Millie is dressed in a qipao, the same as mine, but in bubble-gum pink. She has an apron on top to prevent chocolate crumbs getting on it as she carefully counts all the little cakes she's baked to sell at the Flower Fair. She's made over one hundred mini triple-layered heart-shaped chocolate avocado cakes, her award-winning recipe, and instead of using the money she'll make today to buy a ring light for selfies, she's going to donate it all to a local family literacy charity. She posts a selfie with the cakes encouraging her followers to donate as well.

"Nice one, Millie," I say as I like her post.

Mom nods in approval. "Using your social media platform to do some good in the community. I'm proud of you." She gives Millie's shoulders a little squeeze.

"Smells so delicious," Dad says as he reaches for one of the cakes.

"Dad, hands off!" Millie laughs and shoos him away.

I already packed my mini maple butter tarts in Tupperware containers last night. I like to be prepared. I know I told Millie earlier that I was too busy to bake, but Dev introduced me to this charity in the city that encourages girls to play sports, like field hockey. He's a volunteer coach and he asked if I'd like to help. I said yes and start after the Lunar New Year holidays. So I'm going to donate the proceeds from my tarts to them. I don't think I'll make much money, but from what I learned last weekend on the trail race, every kindness matters.

My phone pings and it's a message from Saskia telling me to save her a maple butter tart and one of Millie's cakes, with an emoji of a smiley face. I send her an emoji back of a smiley face blowing a heart kiss.

We have special permission to drive into school today instead of taking the bus, so Mom and Dad can help us bring in all our baked goods to the gymnasium, where we've set up the fair.

"These games look brilliant," Dad says as we walk by the different stalls with the games the Grade 7s have planned. "Pin the tail on the dragon looks like a winner."

"We made everything ourselves using old cardboard. It was Rainbow's idea."

I point to the backdrop for the photo booth. "She and her eco-art club made that with the stuff that washed up on the beach. Isn't it amazing?" It's a textured mural using plastic bottles, chip bags, bottle caps, foam pieces, and random bits of plastic and glass. It depicts The Great Race, where the twelve winning animals—rat, ox, tiger, rabbit, dragon, snake, horse, goat, monkey, rooster, dog, and pig—are awarded their place in the Chinese Zodiac by the Jade Emperor, the ruler of the heavens.

We find our table, already covered in a festive bright red cloth, and Mom and Dad help us with our display.

"I have a surprise for you both." Mom pulls a large envelope out of her bag and hands it to me.

I open it and pull out a poster to display on our table. In beautiful pink-and-purple script, surrounded by painted cherry blossoms it says, *Baking with Heart, @ Holly-Mei and Millie.*

"Ah-ma painted it. This is just a printout. She'll give the original one to you when she sees you next."

"Look Millie, it even has our Chinese names." I trace my finger over the delicate brushstrokes of 清美, Qing Mei, and 天恩, Tian En.

"I miss Ah-ma," Millie says with an audible sigh.

"Me too." We both stop unpacking our boxes and just stare at the poster. I spoke with Ah-ma after the race last weekend. She said she was so proud of me.

"Even though I didn't win?" I asked.

"Because you help someone without thinking of yourself. That is your strength, baobei," she said. I'm not sure if she's right, but I'd like to keep working on it.

Dad pulls us into a group hug, "Now now, girls, chin up."

"You'll see her before you know it," Mom says with a wink. "Now, back to work. The bell is about to go." She and Dad leave so she can get to the office, and Millie and I hang the poster on the wall above our stand so everyone at the fair will be able to see it.

The Upper School volunteers head down to the gym and get their various stations ready for the influx of Lower School students. At nine o'clock sharp, the Lunar New Year Flower Fair fills with students from all grades, from all backgrounds, and most are dressed in traditional clothes, including the teachers. Both Snowy and Rosie are in fuchsia qipaos and have their hair done up in two side buns. Jinsae and his older sister Seri are in regal hanbok—he in a navy-blue embroidered silk jacket and gray silk pants, she in a turquoise top with rainbow sleeves closed with a pink ribbon that matches her poofy pink skirt. Rhys is in a royal blue silk Chinese-style jacket with gold lining and embroidery. He jokes that he's happy it's a bit big because he plans on winning the dumpling-eating contest. It's amazing to see everyone, even the kids who aren't Asian, dressed to celebrate the biggest holiday in the region.

Millie's and my cakes are selling really well, and we're relieved to take a breather when the students get shooed outside for recess.

"Time for a selfie?" Millie asks. For the past week, she's

stayed away from staged photos and is only posting her real, unfiltered life. Even though the number of likes she gets has dropped, she seems to be less concerned about counting them and more bubbly to be around—basically back to her old self.

"Thought you'd never ask." I laugh as I put my arm around her and we make v-signs as we say "cheese."

"Would you mind if I take a photo of you two for the school paper?" asks Ms. Nguyen, who heads up the *Tai Tam Prep Times*. She's dressed in a red-and-gold traditional Vietnamese ao dai, a long dress which is sort of like a Chinese qipao, but with slits up the waist, with long flowing pants underneath. "It would be great to interview you both after the fair is over. We like to showcase students who do things for the community."

Millie and I both nod our agreement.

"And we can also chat about your sportsmanship medal," Ms. Nguyen says.

"With Saskia too, right?" I ask. I mean, I wouldn't have the medal if it weren't for her. And I wonder if her being in the school paper will help calm her parents, even though it's not the city paper interview the tournament winner got. Saskia told me they had a big talk over the weekend and her parents agreed to let her go to animation camp this summer! She's hoping to learn how to storyboard Esi, her space warrior princess creation. I told her she was going to be as big as Domee Shi, the director of *Turning Red*.

"Yes, of course, Saskia too," Ms. Nguyen says.

Just before noon, we see a group of adults walk together, visiting and inspecting all the stalls in the Flower Fair. I recognize Gemma's mother as the leader. She is a former Hong Kong movie star and has that commanding presence that makes everyone else feel little, even though she is smaller than me. She's also the head of the PTA, so she's always involved in whatever is happening at school.

"These must be the important donors I heard about," Millie whispers in my ear. I immediately correct my posture and stand up straight, my shoulders back, as they approach our table.

"Hello, Holly-Mei," Gemma's mom says.

"Hello, Gemma's mom." I bite my lip because I can't remember her last name but I know it's not the same as Gemma's. She arches an eyebrow. I quickly ask, "Could we offer you a piece of cake or a tart?" Food always puts people in a good mood, and I hope she will take one and move on quickly.

She takes a maple butter tart and places it delicately in her mouth.

"Interesting," she says. I can't tell if that is a good or bad verdict. I suck in my breath as she turns to the group and says, "These are the sisters I told you about." Why was she talking about us? I hope I'm not in trouble. She didn't seem to like me last autumn, especially since I got Gemma and myself locked into the storage shed on the night of the Tsien Wing Opening Gala dress rehearsal and the guards had to rescue us at midnight. Maybe Gemma complained about me and how I'd been behaving, all obsessed with winning the tournament. I bite my lip with worry as she starts to speak.

"To my surprise," she pauses, "they have become good role models for the students." She nods at us and looks back at the group of serious adults. "And are representative of the kind of families we hope to attract to Tai Tam Prep." She gestures for the group to move on to another stand.

"Did Gemma's mom just say nice things about us?" Millie asks.

"Sounds like it," I say, just as confused as she sounds. I scan around and see Gemma looking at us. She puts her thumb up and raises her eyebrows as if she's asking a question. I smile and give her two thumbs-up in return.

The Flower Fair concludes with the much-anticipated lion dance—to scare away evil spirits and bring luck for the New Year. The gym is filled with excited whispers as the students gather in the center of the gym. A drummer starts banging his drum while other musicians clash their cymbals, the vibrations reverberating through the air. A troupe of dancers dressed as lions in brilliant yellow, orange, and red—with one person as the head and front legs and the other as the back legs—delight the crowd with acrobatics. We clap loudly and holler when the lions do seemingly gravity-defying jumps between the narrow podiums, on two legs, and sometimes on all four. Kids clap with glee as the lions blink their wide eyes and pretend to scratch and lick their fur, their little bells tinkling.

In the middle of the dance, the lions walk up to Gemma's mom who feeds them each a bunch of lettuce tied with a red ribbon—the word for lettuce, cai, sounds like the word for wealth. And after the lions pretend to eat it, they spit it back out at the crowd. Some of the students gasp and others giggle. The first time I saw it I thought it was rather rude, but the lions are actually spreading wealth and luck to everyone. The lions end their dance with the loud crackling of pretend firecrackers and the unfurling of a banner that reads 恭喜發財, while the musicians shout out "Gong Hei Fat Choy" to wish us all a prosperous New Year.

At the end of the school day, I help pack up the Flower Fair stalls, games, and decorations with all my friends, except for Rhys, who is napping in the corner after winning the dumpling-eating competition. I think back to my perfect plan—to get things to how they were before the break. It turns out the plan had more ups and downs than the Hair Raiser at Ocean Park. But as I look at all of us, in our beautiful Asian-style clothes, I can confidently say that we are even better friends than before.

# 21

The sun sets over the plaza at Repulse Bay Beach, where we've all come after school. Still in our traditional clothes, we hungrily devour burgers and bubble tea, celebrating the end of a fantastic Flower Fair and the start of our Lunar New Year holiday.

"Woohoo, we have ten days off school," Henry says.

"And we get red laisee packets," Rhys says as he rubs two fingers together to indicate money. Rosie gives him a gentle slap on the arm and rolls her eyes.

"Anyone going away?" Gemma asks the table but then answers her own question. "We're doing the first three days of the New Year here, you know, all the visiting with family stuff, then we're off to the Maldives for the rest of the break."

"We're going back to Seoul to visit my grandmother—she's going to get a kick out of this." Jinsae flashes his K-pop dance-off champion certificate.

"We're going to go hiking in Taiwan, in Taroko Gorge," Rainbow says.

My ears perk up. "You are? I haven't been there in ages." My family went when I was eight. "You have to give me all the good tips, especially for snacks, okay? For when we go in the spring." I was so excited when I found out that all the Upper School kids get to go on an Experience Week trip in Asia. We get to choose where we go and I chose Taiwan, because it reminds me of Ah-ma.

"What about you, Theo?" Gemma asks.

"We're staying here. We always spend it with my grandmother and she's getting too old to travel. But it's super fun with her. Except she likes to cut my hair to cut away the year's bad luck herself." They all laugh and reminisce about Theo's lopsided haircut from last year. "And she makes the best dumplings." He smiles, his dimples on show.

"Ahem, no way. My Ah-ma makes the best dumplings," I joke and laugh. But my smile soon fades.

"Are you okay?" Dev asks, touching my elbow.

"Yes, fine." I shrug. "Just missing my grandmother. It's going to be my first Chinese New Year without her."

As I get ready for bed that night, I rummage through my

drawers and find Ah-ma's scarf that I sneakily brought with me to Hong Kong as a souvenir. It still smells like her—a mix of Tiger Balm and lavender. I put it on my pillow and fall into a deep, dream-filled sleep.

In my dream, I wake up to a knock on my bedroom door. It's Ah-ma coming into my bedroom in Toronto, sitting on my bed, and stroking my hair.

"Baobei, wake up."

I roll over and pull the pillow over my head to block out the sun so I don't have to get up yet. I don't want this dream to end.

Then I feel someone shaking my shoulders. I pull the pillow off my head, annoyed, and say, "What?"

"Zaoshang hao, baobei," a gentle voice says. It's not Mom, Dad, or Joy, and certainly not Millie. I rub my eyes and open them wide.

It's Ah-ma!

Wait, what? Am I still dreaming?

"Are you really here?" I ask, grabbing her hand and putting it to my cheek. She's warm, just like her laughter at my question.

"Yes, I am here."

I bolt straight up in bed and scan my room. I'm still in Hong Kong. And Ah-ma is in my Hong Kong bedroom.

She must register my confusion because she says, "Surprise visit. Your mama and baba arrange."

"This is the best New Year's present ever!" I bury my face into her neck and keep it there for six months' worth of hugs.

After breakfast, Ah-ma hands me a broom. "Come, so much to do today. Tomorrow is Lunar New Year Eve, so we have to prepare."

I smile and push the broom as I say, "Sweep the bad luck away."

In the afternoon, the whole family gets in the van to go to the city. We've always celebrated Lunar New Year in Toronto but spending it in Hong Kong is extra amazing. It's the biggest festival of the year and the city is bursting with red-and-gold decorations. You can feel the excitement about the holiday in the air, like the anticipation of Christmas back home.

Our destination is Victoria Park in Causeway Bay, where all the basketball courts and soccer pitches have been turned into the biggest Lunar New Year Flower Market in the city. Families shop together for plants and flowers, which are said to bring luck and good fortune into the home. There are stalls of white-and-purple orchids, anthurium with red shiny flowers, and large branches of pink peach blossoms.

"Look at these!" Millie points to a lucky bamboo tree, twirled like a curly straw. "This is giving me an idea for a new dessert."

"Can we get one of those trees with the miniature oranges?" I ask.

"Those are kumquat. Look like little balls of gold," Ah-ma explains. "Can make jam with the fruit later."

"And candy," Millie says.

"Cool," I say. Candy is way more interesting than jam.

Just outside the park in the alleys of Tin Hau, we pick up some red paper cutouts to stick on the windows. They all say fu, which means good fortune.

"Remember girls, we need to placing them like this," Ah-ma turns the paper so that the Chinese character is upside down, "to make sure fu will fall into the house."

"Don't forget about these." Millie picks up a pack of laisee lucky money red envelopes and hands them to Ah-ma. "Make sure Mom and Dad fill them nice and thick!"

We laugh and Ah-ma pats Millie on the arm before putting the laisee packs back on the shelf. We don't argue with her just in case we don't get any lucky money later.

We pass a quiet evening at home. Ah-ma insists in vain on starting her famous jiaozi, *dumplings*, but Mom says we can do that together tomorrow. "Xiuxi, xiuxi," she says, *rest, rest*. Ah-ma reluctantly agrees and shuffles away from the kitchen in the slippers she brought from home.

The next afternoon, we all follow Ah-ma into the kitchen to start preparing the dumplings for our feast tonight—it's something we do together every year. From the fridge she pulls out the dough that she made in the morning. Millie flours the countertop and starts kneading the dough. Then she puts a hole in the middle and starts stretching it, like a giant doughnut.

"Is this wide enough?" she asks. Ah-ma nods her approval as she paces behind us, like a master chef watching her sous-chefs at work. Then Millie starts cutting the doughnut into one-inch pieces and in her palm shapes them into round balls.

I pull out a small rolling pin and start rolling the dough balls.

"Remember you need to turning," Ah-ma says, demonstrating how to rotate each little pancake ninety degrees after every roll. Soon I have a stack of perfectly round dumpling wrappers in a little pile. She nods and pats me on the head to indicate approval and flour from her hand falls down on me like snow.

On the other side of the counter, Dad chops the cabbage, ginger, and scallions, and puts them into a big bowl and Mom mixes them into the minced meat with a pair of wooden chopsticks.

"Feichang hao," Ah-ma says, *very good*. She claps her hands as she surveys the prepped ingredients. "Now wrapping time."

This is my favorite part. We sit around the dining room table, each one of us stuffing and wrapping our dumplings that will be cooked together in one pan. We're doing things separately but all for a common goal: a delicious feast.

We watch Ah-ma as she closes the stuffed dumpling with pleats along the top.

"We close them this way so they looking like ancient gold ingots," she says.

"To wish everyone wealth for the New Year," Mom says.

We soon all have a plateful of perfectly pleated dumplings, except Dad, whose dumplings all burst open. "Aiya, Peter! Too much filling," Ah-ma says.

At six o'clock, our doorbell rings. It's Rosie, Rhys, Auntie Helen, and Uncle Charlie. We greet each other with "Xin Nian Kuai Le" and "Gong Xi Fa Cai", *Happy New Year* and *Wish You Prosperity*. Millie and I wear our new qipaos and Rosie and Rhys are in Chinese dress too. Ah-ma takes photos of all the cousins with her iPad.

"I hear you are Tai Tam Prep dumpling eating champion." Ah-ma pats Rhys's shoulder. "We will have plenty of dumplings tonight," she says with a wink.

After a dinner of dumplings and steamed fish—the word for fish, yu, sounds the same as the word for abundance, meaning we'll have an abundance of things in the new year—Ah-ma brings out dessert: nian gao. Like everything else on the table, it has a double meaning. Nian means *year* and gao means both *cake* and *tall*—which will hopefully represent the tall luck we'll have next year. I bite into the freshly pan-fried cake. It's a bit crispy on the outside and gooey soft on the inside.

"It was all so delicious, but I couldn't eat another bite," Rosie says with a big exhale.

"It's okay, I'll have your piece," Rhys says as he takes the cake off her plate. "What?" he asks when everyone laughs.

Millie and I clear the dishes and the adults have their after-dinner drinks, then it's time for mahjong. We split into two groups—the kids sit on the floor to play at the coffee table with a sparkly-turquoise set while the adults set up their game on a foldable card table with a jade-green set. A wonderful loud click-clack sound fills the room as the tiles are shuffled.

Ah-ma floats around, giving hints on moves to secure a pong, kong, or chow, all different ways to have winning hands, kind of like gin rummy, where you have sets of identical tiles of sequential numbers in a suit.

"Who's winning?" Dad calls from the adult table.

"We're not keeping score," Rosie says over her shoulder.

"We're just having fun," I say. Ah-ma nods and smiles. I yell out "kong" and take Rhys's discarded bamboo tile to make a matching set of the number eight.

I trace my finger over the bamboo stalks carved into the tile. Ah-ma said bamboo is strong but flexible. I think back to what Ah-ma said before, about knowing myself, including my strengths and weaknesses. After these past few weeks, I've finally learned that I can plan as much as I want, and even if I think it's the most perfect plan in the entire world, I still need to be flexible. Like bamboo, swaying in the wind, but firmly planted.

★ ★ ★ ★ ★

# ACKNOWLEDGMENTS

It was such a delight to dive back into Holly-Mei's world to bring readers Book 2 in the series. I couldn't have done it without the following people, to whom I send a huge thank you and a massive hug:

Claire Stetzer, my editor at Inkyard Press, for helping me tell the best version of Holly-Mei's newest adventure in Hong Kong. And to Yao Xiao, Carla Weise, Alexandra Niit, Gigi Lau, and the Inkyard Press design team for bringing Holly-Mei and her friends to life with the beautiful cover and interior illustrations.

Carrie Pestritto, my wonderful agent, for encouraging me to write middle-grade—a genre where my heart has found a home.

The Hong Kong University MFA Class of 2020 alumni writing group for helping me tease out the themes and conflicts in the book. You made the story richer with your keen writers' eyes. I am grateful for your friendship and support: Mariella Candela, Fung Ying Cheng, Christy Hirai, Tom K. E. Chan, Kelly Chan, Gabrielle Tsui, Dr. Shivani Salil, and Jenny Ho Chang.

The SCBWI Hong Kong chapter, particularly the TST group for your gentle guidance when critiquing my opening chapters: Mio Debnam, Rachel Ip, Laura Mannering, Sarah Rose, Karla Sy, Michelle Fung, and Ritu Hemnani.

To my HKFC D-team Core for helping me keep my link to the wonderful city of Hong Kong, so I could be there in spirit: Aisling Dwyer (mother of the real Saskia), Katie Daly, Katy Spooner, Helen Dowding, and especially Ellie Poulton for your Peak Master hiking knowledge. To the fantastic HKFC field hockey players for helping me better understand competition, pressure, and all things related to the sport: Jess Boa, Beatrice Furniss, Simon Chapman, Dev Dillon, and Katy Mountain. To Caroline Drewett for your help understanding the mindset of pushy parents. To Ken Chow for making me do early runs along the boardwalk and encouraging me to jump into the South China Sea. To Lindsay Ernst for taking me on open water swims outside the shark net (despite the jellyfish) and for inspiring the swim race. To Liz Chow for coming up with the tastiest recipes in the back of the book. To Rachel Middagh for keeping me up to date on tween life with daily memes. To Zoe Belhomme and Melvin Byres for helping me research the city race and letting me use the Dragon Dash name. To Violet Middagh and Shasya Shinde for your insights into middle-school life. To Anthea Murray for talking to me about being part of a mixed-Ghanaian family and inspiring Saskia's heritage. To Susan Blumberg-Kason for your continued cheerleading.

And finally, to my family, whose pride in my work fuels my passion. To my sister, Natalie, for your constant support and inspiration. Thank you for being the Millie to my Holly-Mei. To Elsa for your keen editing eye and for helping me keep the dialogue real. To Sandor for devouring the book and telling me it was good, no notes. And to Jukka for your silent but ever-present support.

# GLOSSARY

Chinese and English are the official languages of Hong Kong. Cantonese is the predominant form of Chinese in the city. Mandarin, the official language of Mainland China, is now heard more frequently on the streets of Hong Kong and forms part of the local school curriculum. Cantonese and Mandarin words share the same traditional characters (used in Hong Kong and Taiwan, whilst Mainland China uses simplified characters), but have different pronunciation. Taiwanese is also a distinct language and is spoken widely on the island of Taiwan, particularly in the south, where my mother and her family are from.

Below are the Chinese words found in the book in traditional characters with their definitions. The words are in Mandarin Chinese, except where noted, and include the pinyin tone marks, which indicate the pitch of the word. The same syllable pronounced with a different tone has a completely different meaning. Mandarin has four tones. For simplicity, only Mandarin tones are noted.

For example:

1st tone—ā:

the *a* is said in a steady, high pitch. As in 媽 mā *mother*

2nd tone—á:

the *a* is said in a rising pitch, like you are asking a question. As in 麻 má *linen*

3rd tone—ǎ:

the *a* is said in a dipping tone that falls and rises again. As in 馬 mǎ *horse*

4th tone—à:

the *a* is said with a sharp drop from high to low. As in 傌 mà *to scold*

## SAYINGS

**Baobei** 寶貝 **bǎobèi** [bow (as in take a bow) bay]:
*treasure, darling*

**Mm goi** 唔該 [mm goy (as in boy)]:
*Cantonese for thank you, please, and excuse me*

**Zi zhi zhi ming** 自知之明 **zì zhī zhī míng** [ze jer jer ming]:
*to know oneself, to have self-awareness*

**Fu** 福 **fú** [foo]:
*good fortune*

**Zaoshang hao** 早上好 **zǎoshang hǎo** [zow (as in how)
shahng how]: *good morning*

**Feichang hao** 非常好 **fēicháng hǎo** [fay chahng how]:
*very good*

**Xiuxi** 休息 **xiūxi** [she-oo-she]:
*to rest*

**Xin nian kuai le** 新年快樂 **xīn nián kuài lè** [shin nee-an
kwai le]: *happy new year*

**Gongxi facai** 恭喜發財 **gōngxǐ fācái** [gong she fa tsai]:
*wishing you a prosperous new year.* Gong hei fat choy *is the
Cantonese equivalent*

# PEOPLE

**Ah-ma** 阿嬤 [ah mah]:
*Taiwanese for grandmother, either father's mother or mother's
mother*

**Ah-gong** 阿公 [ah gong]:
*Taiwanese for grandfather, either father's father or mother's father*

**Maa maa** 嫲嫲 [ma ma (with long a sounds)]:
*Cantonese for father's mother*

**Po po** 婆婆 [pahw pahw]:
*Cantonese for mother's mother*

# FOOD

**Huoguo** 火鍋 **huǒguō** [hwo gwo]:
*hot pot, a dish where you cook your own ingredients in a shared broth*

**Sa yong** 沙翁 [sa yong]:
*Cantonese for fried sugar egg puffs*

**Xiao long bao** 小籠包 **xiǎo lóng bāo** [she-ow long bow (as in take a bow)]: *steamed dumplings filled with meat and broth, also called soup dumplings*

**Dandan mian** 擔擔麵 **dàndan miàn** [dan dan mee-an]:
*noodles in a spicy peanut broth*

**Jiaozi** 餃子 **jiǎozi** [gee-ow ze]:
*dumplings*

**Yu** 魚 **yú** [yu (as in the French tu)]:
*fish*

**Nian gao** 年糕 **nián gāo** [nee-an gow (as in how)]:
*a pan-fried rice cake served at Chinese New Year*

# CANDY CANE-WHITE RABBIT CHIP COOKIES

This recipe combines two of my favorite childhood treats—peppermint candy canes and White Rabbit candies. You can find White Rabbit candies in your local Chinese grocery store.

## INGREDIENTS

1 ¼ cups all-purpose flour
¾ cup non-salted butter
¾ cup chopped White Rabbit candy
(chocolate chip-sized chunks)
½ cup crushed candy canes (optional extra for dipping)
1 tsp salt
¼ cup white sugar
¼ cup brown sugar
¼ tsp baking soda
¼ tsp baking powder
1 egg (at room temperature)
½ tsp vanilla extract

**Makes 24 cookies**

1. Preheat oven to 180C (350F).

2. Whisk together the flour, baking soda, baking powder, and salt.

3. Beat the butter, sugar, and egg, then add the vanilla.

4. Slowly add the flour mixture.

5. Add the White Rabbit chips and crushed candy canes and mix with a spatula.

6. Place the cookie dough on a parchment-lined cookie sheet (approximately 2 tbsp each).

7. Dip each ball of cookie dough into a dish of crushed candy canes.

8. Chill on baking sheet for 10 minutes in the fridge.

9. Bake for about 12 minutes.

10. Allow to cool before moving from cookie sheet.

# MILLIE'S CHOCOLATE AVOCADO CAKE

This moist and fluffy cake can be made with just one bowl. I like to use unsweetened raspberry or apricot jam between the layers of cake. The cake is even better covered with Chocolate Avocado frosting!

## CAKE

### INGREDIENTS

1 ½ cups white sugar
2 cups all-purpose flour
¾ cup unsweetened cocoa powder
1 ½ tsp baking powder
1 ½ tsp baking soda
1 tsp salt
2 avocados (about 1 ½ cups) mashed until very smooth
1 cup milk
¼ cup vegetable oil
2 tsp vanilla extract
1 cup boiling water

1. Preheat oven to 180 C (350 F). Grease and flour 2 (or 3) 8" cake tins.

2. Combine dry ingredients into a mixing bowl.

3. Add wet ingredients except boiling water. Mix on medium until smooth (about 2 minutes). Add boiling water and mix until combined.

4. Bake the cakes for 25-30 minutes (less if making 3 layers) until a cake tester comes out clean.

5. Cool in the pans for 10 minutes and then remove; continue cooling on a wire rack.

# FROSTING

## INGREDIENTS

*2 large avocados, soft*
*¼ cup unsweetened cocoa*
*½ cup maple syrup (Canadian!)*
*1 tsp vanilla extract*

Combine all ingredients in a mixing bowl and mix until smooth. If you find the frosting too thick, add a tablespoon of milk at a time until it reaches the desired consistency.

Remember to wait until the cake is cool to the touch before frosting it.